Doing His Time

Who Said Dating A Baller Was Easy?

by:
Nichelle Walker

®

A *NWHoodTales Novel.*
Published by NWHoodTales
P.O Box 804782 Chicago IL, 60680

Second Edition

This book is a work of fiction. Names, characters, places and incidents are products of the author's imagination or are used fictitiously. Any resemblance to actual events or locales or person, living or dead, is entirely coincidental.

Library of Congress Cataloging-in-Publication Data;
2007902281

ISBN-13: 978-0-9794028-1-4

ISBN-10: 0-9794028-1-6

Publishing Consultation: Nakea S. Murray - Literary Consultant Group

www.nwhoodtales.com

Doing His Time Book Reviews

⭐⭐⭐⭐⭐ **OH YES SHE DID!**

By <u>OOSA Online Book Club "O.O.S.A."</u>

In DOING HIS TIME, written by debut author Nichelle Walker, we're in Chicago , where we meet Emerald, a frantic sixteen year old celebrating her birthday. While parking lot pimping with her girls, she meets and greets Dollar, a bona fide hustler, who she is looking forward to getting to know.

As Dollar and Emerald get more acquainted, Emerald loses her modesty and begins stepping on and over people as she rises to the top. Be careful who you step on as you may have to come down that same unpaved road.

Emerald learns valuable lessons about love and loyalty while DOING HIS TIME. I for one cannot wait for part two. Nichelle is definitely an author on the rise and this is a book that all book junkies will enjoy.

★★★★★ **Who Can You Trust?,**

<u>Real Divas of Literature Book Club</u>

To all the ladies that think that a man is the only way to live the glamorous life then this is the book for you. Nichelle takes us into the world of Emerald who is dying to meet a baller that can take her away from her poor life style. Then there is Dollar, a well named drug lord who spots Emerald and instantly wants to give her the best thing in life but Dollar has a little more up his sleeve then Emerald knows about. He claims to love her and all he wants is to make her happy but the streets is his life and that's all he knows and all he cares about. When Emerald is arrested for being a mule for the man she loved, she soon finds out who the real Dollar is and all the scandalous things that he has done. She sets out on revenge on Dollar and on a family who she thought would never betray her.

This was a very good novel that Nichelle put together and I can not wait until Part 2 hits the shelves.

⭐⭐⭐⭐⭐ Doing His Time

Shay C "PeoplewholoveGoodBooks"

Emerald wishes for the finer things in life....things that only a man with deep, deep pockets can afford. When she meets Dollar, he sweeps her off her feet and gives Emerald everything she wants and more. Alienated from her family and friends, Emerald is soon caught up and in over her head. She has no idea what Dollar has in store for her. Soon Dollar uses Emerald's love for him to control and manipulate her and against her better judgment, Emerald makes a decision that lands her in jail and may forever change her life. At first Emerald is still Dollar's down for whatever chick and determined to "do his time" but all that changes when an unexpected betrayal comes to light and Emerald is forced to grow up and hell hath no fury for a woman scorned! Doing His Time is an impressive debut by Nichelle Walker. A fast-paced, drama-filled juicy story that once you start reading, you won't put it down until the very last page! A fresh, new voice in Urban Fiction....Nichelle Walker is a Author on the rise! Can't wait to read Part 2!

This book is dedicated to everyone that has a dream, never give up. Dreams do come true!

Acknowledgments

When I sat down to write my thank you's, it was a lot harder than I thought I have so many people to thank. First I would like to thank God for blessing me with this precious gift, I know through him I can do all things. I would like to thank my mom for being such a strong woman and an inspiration to me. To my sister and nephews I love ya'll to death you're the best sister in the whole wide world. To my step father thanks for all the long talks. I like to especially thank my grandmother for being the back bone of our family thanks for always being there for us.

To all my uncles and aunties it's so many of ya'll I love you all so much and thanks for being the best uncle and aunties a girl could have. To all my cousin I love each and every one of you (those I know) I'm glad we all get along and we can go out and kick it with each other.

To my Cuzo Boo I want you to know I love you so much, you're the brother I never had. Thanks for being so hard and me and Nicole and keeping us outta these streets. Lords knows where we would be if you wasn't so hard on us. Thanks for protecting us. I can't wait for you to come home so we can kick it hard hold ya head up. And to all my family I will see you on 95th street at the park for the family reunion this year. (Ha-ha)

To my inspiration Keon and my little momma Skyy you two keep me on tha grind I love you both with all my heart. To my god daughter Eriyonna god mommy loves you very much. Lil Eric stay sweet, Francis thanks for the years we shared I wish you nothing but the best, you're a wonderful father. Thanks for copping me my first computer and printer. You've always been supportive of me and my dreams from day one. When I told you I wanted to be a writer you made sure I had everything I needed. I want to thank you for your continue support much love Nicey.

To Ms Avilez you're a wonderful person and the best grandma in the whole wide world. Thanks for always being there for me and your grandchildren we love you very much. Barabra Ann, Amanda and Ikwan stay sweet thanks for always keeping me laughing.

Thanks to the entire Thurman family it's to many of ya'll to name. Mutt thank you for showing me how to put my talent down on paper, you're very talented and I know your day is coming soon! Thanks for the computer program I blazed this book in, I owe you one, and Kim you better read my book ☺ I love ya'll.

Torrian Ferguson thanks for helping me get my name out in the literary world. Thanks for being so kind and giving me words of encouragement. You showed me how to get from point A to point B thanks for everything. Thanks to Keith at Marion Designs for a slamming book cover. Also I will like to thank Amanda Jacques for hooking up my company logo she's to hot.

To my new publicist Nakea S. Murray, boy you stepped in and re-upped my project. Now it's better than ever, your wisdom and grind is undeniable. Thanks for believing in me and in *Doing His Time,* now I'm ready to grind hard, together were gonna make history.

To my home skillet Dreana, what can I say you're the best friend a girl could have, you keep me laughing. Thanks for always being there through thick or thin. I can't imagine not having you as my friend, Thanks for always supporting me and my dreams look at me now, we riding for life best friends 4 ever I love you!

To my other girlfriends ride or die, I know I worried ya'll, nagged and probably got on ya'll nerves about this project. Thanks for understanding me and no matter what giving me your honest opinion. Even when I was freaking out about this project you guys held me together. I had ya'll reading especially you Dreana but what are friends for ☺ I love you all. Dreana, Tasha, Denise (we've been down since the crest I love you very much), Alecia, Sonya, Nicole and Shay *we so blue* together **PYT**.

To all my P2K homies from the VZW Ivan, Taye, Vera, Janell (what's up J-Rock get at me), Terrence (Tee), Jason, Mr Thames (Thanks for always encouraging me to write my book and letting me know I can make the Essence best seller list one day look out for me) Velma, Tanisha, Tasha, Sheila, and Dreana. This is a long way from them soul food scripts I use to pass around. I love ya'll thanks for believing in me first and having my back I got ya'll. And also I want to thank Veronica, (what's up V) Bernard (I miss laughing with yo crazy self) shit it's so many of ya'll I'll be days naming people. To all my peeps at VZW thanks for holding ya girl down good looking out.

Thanks to my god mother Wendy look at me now, Hi Pam and the whole Shiloh Temple family. Thanks goes out to the Bailey family, the Payton family and the Avilez (Burrage) family.

And to the special people, who believed in me the most, saw my vision and understood my dream. Thank you for believing in me without you this would not be a reality. And to everybody I forgot to name please blame my mind and not my heart. Ya'll know I got a memory problem. So if I forgot you it was not on purpose, I still love you. RIP Percy Thomas SR. I know you would be proud of me granddad, I miss you, we all miss you.

Last but not least to all the *HATERS* keep hatin and I'ma keep shinning on that ass *I Luv it!*

To all the book stores that stocked my book thank you. To all my readers that coped this book thank you I wouldn't be nothing without you. Now sit back, relax and kick yo feet up because this shit right here is on fire.

Peace

Tha Princess of HoodTales

Nichelle,

NWHoodTales We Keep Them Pages Turning.

Them Pages Turning

Tha Good Life!

Close your eyes and picture a life of never having to want for anything. A life where you're rolling in the hottest whips, rocking the hottest bags, living in the fliest cribs, and overnight stays at the finest hotels. Picture a life where you never have to wear the same thing twice. A life where you take trips to change the bad weather. A life where you're hated by most and envied by all.

Picture tha good life, a life of taking five figure shopping sprees anytime you wish. A life most bitches would love to have; a life of spending money like water. Picture the life of a baller's bitch.

Now, open your eyes and read the struggle, because being a baller's bitch ain't easy.

Peace,
Emerald
Doing His Time.

Prologue

Usually seconds turn into minutes, minutes turn into hours, hours turn into days, and days turn into months. When you're out living your life, time flies by. But where I'm at, time moves slowly, like a hundred-year-old lady crossing the street. It takes forever for a week to pass, and it feels like years before the month ends. As the days slowly pass, I get more depressed. I try to sleep, but wind up staying awake, staring at these cold gray walls.

I'm used to a certain lifestyle. I got accustomed to the finer things in life. I was a baller's bitch. I never coped nothing but the best of everything. Now I'm sleeping under nasty-ass used sheets and they make me cringe; my skin's flaking up from using that generic-ass soap these crackers give me.

I thought being a baller's bitch was easy. I had the hottest whips, the best clothes, and mad dollars at my fingertips. I was the baddest bitch in the CHI. I was Dollar's girl. And I was his wifey, not no sideline ho. I enjoyed being a baller's chick, but everything that glitters ain't gold.

I was down for Dollar. I talked to him every day since I was sixteen, and now it's been three months since I saw him or heard a word from him. Dis nigga is playing me now. I'm the same bitch that went across state lines for him, took the stand and lied for him; I'm the same woman he asked to marry him three months ago. Now a bitch can't even get a visit outta his ass after all I did for him.

"Everybody up and out!" the prison guard yells.

I couldn't jump up fast enough. I ran down the hall because I need to be the first person on the phone. Once I made it to the head of the line, I couldn't dial Sissy's number fast enough. I need to see what the hell is going on.

Sissy answers right away. "Emerald, how you holding up?" Sissy asks.

"Bitch, how you think? I'm in fucking prison! Where the fuck is Dollar? How come he ain't put no money on my books or came and seen me?"

Sissy swallows hard before she answers me. "I been trying to call him," she says in a low voice. "I don't know if he got locked up or not."

"Bitch, *what the fuck you mean you ain't heard from him?*" I scream so loud my voice begins to shake. "What about S.L.? You call him."

"Emerald, I done tried everybody," she cries.

"What?"

"I don't know what's going on."

"Call his momma right now!" I ordered her.

Sissy clicks over, calls Dollar's momma on the three-way, and clicks me in.

"Hello, Sissy. Dollar ain't in," Dollar's momma says.

Sissy cuts her off. "Ms. Price, I have Emerald on the line."

"What's going on, Ms. Price?" I ask. "I'm in here and I haven't heard or seen Dollar in three months now!"

"Baby, I ain't seen him either," his momma says. "I think he out of town. I'll tell him to come up there soon as he gets back."

"What am I supposed to do for money?"

"I got some," Sissy answers. "I'll put some on your books."

"Well, I need for you to come today," I said.

"All right. See you when I get there."

I hung up the phone—there were too many people behind me waiting to make phone calls. My gut keeps telling me something's going on with Dollar. My gut tells me that he was playing me. He done got me locked up, and now *I'm doing his time*.

Chapter 1
DOLLAR

It was hot as hell in the CHI today. 79th and Stony Island was gonna be on and popping tonight. This was early heat for Chicago—it's the beginning of June—but when it's hot outside, that equals niggas and rides. Tonight's my sixteenth birthday, and me and my girls are gonna be living it up.

Me and my younger sister Sissy are only nine months apart; my momma was popping us outta her coochie as fast as she could. We live with our grandma. Our father went to jail when I was just three years old, and our mother passed away that same year as well. Grandma would never tell us what happened to our mother; all we knew was that she was killed.

"Emerald, can I come with y'all?" Sissy asked.

"No! You too young," I answered.

"You only nine months older than me."

My sister and me could pass for twins. Our mother was Filipino, and our father was 100% black. I filled out quicker than Sissy, but we both had gray eyes and long curly hair. Our lips were nice and full, and we some redbones. I was shaped like a Coke bottle, while Sissy had yet to fill out but it was only a matter of time before Sissy came into herself.

"Sissy, I ain't got time for you to be no scaredy-cat tonight."

"I ain't gone be."

"Fine, then." I pulled out the latest outfit I had purchased from the local cheap clothing store, Rave. It was all I could afford, but I ain't tripping cuz whatever I put on, I'ma stand out cuz I'm fly.

"Let me see what you wearing, Sissy," I said.

Sissy held up a wrinkled outfit and some busted sandals.

"Where the hell you think you going looking like that?"

"What's the matter?" Sissy asked.

"Everything!" There was no way Sissy was fitting into my shorts, but we were the same bra size. I pulled out one of my sexy shirts, ran a iron over Sissy's wrinkled shorts, and handed her a pair of my sandals.

Once we got dressed, I got the keys to Grandma's Ford Mustang and headed over to Me Me's house. Me Me was my best friend. I've known her since the first grade; that's my bitch, we do everything together. Me Me was a redbone and just as pretty as me, so we was always shittin' on dem hating bitches.

"What's up, bitch?" Me Me yelled as she opened her front door.

"Nothing. You ready?"

"Yeah. Why you bring Tattletale wit' ya?"

"Forget you, Me Me," Sissy said as she rolled her eyes.

"She cool," I said. "Is them bitches gone be ready when we get there? You know I gots to be in by one."

"Yeah, they waiting on us."

Once we got into the car, we had one last stop over to Alicia's crib to pick up her and Tasha. Alicia and Tasha were cousins, and they completed our clique. Once everyone was in, we headed full speed to 79th and Stony Island to see what was poppin.

"Shit, the niggas gone be out tonight!" Me Me yelled, popping her fingers to the sounds of Trina's CD *Da Baddest Bitch*.

"I know, and it's my birthday, so I get first pick over you bitches," I replied.

As the strip pulled closer, the more eager we got to pull up and park. The block was packed like we knew it would be; all you heard was niggas' sounds banging 50's new CD *The Massacre*. Chrome rims and nice whips everywhere. It was a lot of bitches jocking the niggas, but ain't nobody hurting the CHI like me. I can make a man change his mind and come and holla at me if I wanted him.

We parked in the Sears parking lot and walked down toward the White Castle to find some action. Plenty of niggas was trying to holla at me, but I wasn't looking for no passenger seat nigga.

Once we made it to the parking lot, it was packed tight. The Monte Carlo club was out; all the car clubs was out tonight. But one whip stood out to me: a money-green 745 BMW. It had 24-inch Choppers, the paint was candy-colored, and the chrome grill made the car stand out in the crowd. I wanted to know whose ride that was. I could see myself with that nigga, that's a good look to me.

"Damn, bitch, you see that shit?" I moaned as I pointed at the 745.

"Yeah, that's fly. Go and holla," said Me Me.

"What? No way."

"Well, I'ma go and holla," Me Me said.

As she tried to take off, I pulled her stank ass back. "Bitch, didn't I tell you I get first pick?"

"Well, go and holla."

And I was. When I turned around, a fine, tall dark chocolate brother with pretty white teeth was standing in my face. I sized him up. He was paid; he smelled like money; he was rocking the latest Sean John outfit with some fresh Air Ones. His wrist was frostbit minus two degrees, his chain was hanging low, and he had the latest Jacob on. His low-cut fade had deep waves like Indian hair. His nails were manicured, and his skin didn't have a bump in sight.

He smelled great; his scent hit you before he did. He was sexy, and he was the one I wanted to talk to.

"I saw you pointing at my car," he said.

"Oh, I was actually pointing at some-thing else, not your car." I smiled. Arrogant and bold. I love a nigga that's sure of himself.

"I'm Dollar," he said as he held out his hand for a shake.

"Emerald."

"That's a pretty name for a pretty girl."

"Thank you."

"What you doing out tonight?"

"It's my birthday, so me and my girls are just kicking it," I said.

"Happy birthday. Can I get your number?" he asked.

"Well, I ain't got no cell phone, but I can give you my house phone number."

"No cell phone? This is the new age."

I knew he was right. I didn't have money to pay for a cell phone, but I wanted to get Dollar's number bad. "Well, give me yours and I'll make sure to call you," I said.

Dollar wrote his number down on a piece of paper and handed it to me. I wanted Dollar to want me, so I stuffed his number into my purse, turned around, and walked away slowly. I wanted Dollar to see my plump ass.

"Is he looking?" I asked Me Me.

"Girl, yeah."

After the night grew old and we had a pocketful of numbers, I looked at my watch and saw that it was getting late. I knew if I came in late, Grandma wouldn't let me use the car again.

As we walked down to the car, I saw Dollar stop in his 745 and holla my name. I gave Sissy the keys and walked over to see what Dollar wanted.

"What's up?" I asked him, bending over into the driver's side of the car.

"You want to get something to eat?" he asked.

I wanted to say yeah, but there was no way I could go and get something to eat when I had less than a hour to be back in the house. "No. I got to drop my girls off."

"I could follow you and then you could get in the car with me," he said.

That sounded tempting, but Big Momma didn't play, and I wasn't trying to be on lockdown. "Look, how about you come get me in the morning from the Walgreens on 79th at eight o'clock?" I suggested.

"I can't come to your crib."

I just looked at him with my "you're playing" face.

"A'ight," Dollar moaned. "Can I give you a birthday kiss at least?"

I put my head into the car and kissed Dollar softly on the lips. I felt a tingle go through my body. I knew I was ready for Dollar.

I waved goodbye to Dollar as he drove away, hoping that he would pick me up the next day.

Chapter 2
SPOILED

I woke up early to prepare for my date. After a quick lie to Grandma telling her I was kicking it with Me Me for the day, I soaked my body in Victoria's Secret Pear scent to make sure I was smelling good. I pulled out a pair of jeans from the Rainbow, a nice tank top, and a pair of flip flops to match. I knew my taste in clothes was not going to be up to Dollar's standards, but what could I do? I could only afford what I could.

I made up my face, grabbed my bus card, caught the first bus smoking to the Walgreens, and waited outside for Dollar to pull up.

Fifteen minutes later, Dollar pulled up in a brand-new Yukon sitting on the biggest rims I'd ever seen. He jumped out the car, gave me a big hug and a kiss, and handed me a dozen roses.

"Thank you!" I said.

"Anything for you, cutie." Dollar opened the door for me.

I got in, and we pulled off. Dollar admired my beauty; I noticed him staring at me when we stopped at a light.

Dollar was smoother than a baby's ass. His charisma was sharp. He knew all the right things to say and when to say them. His cologne smelled great; I could tell that scent anywhere. He had on Kenneth Cole Black. The lil boyz at my school wore that same cologne, but it smelled much better on him. Dollar was a fine piece of chocolate, and I was ready for a taste.

"What's your real name?" I asked him.

Dollar looked at me and flashed his pretty smile. He kind of reminded me of Tyrese's sexy ass. "My government name is Vonzel Miller. And you?"

"My name is Emerald. Emerald Jones."

"So where you wanna go?" Dollar asked me.

"It don't matter."

Dollar took me shopping. He could tell by my clothes that I was used to shopping at the Pick N' Save, and his ladies wore nothing but the best.

First he took me to the BEBE store. I'd never been in there before, and now I knew why: everything I liked was over 60 dollars. I was embarrassed because I couldn't afford name-brand stuff like this. Dollar told me to pick whatever I wanted.

"I can't afford anything in here," I said.

"I'm buying. It's for your birthday."

I heard him loud and clear and wanted to grab everything I seen. But Dollar's a street nigga, and bitches come a dime a dozen to him. I ain't trying to be his sideline ho. I know sometimes these niggas will fuck with you and try to test you to see if you a hood rat, so I put on a act like I was scared to pick out something. I wanted Dollar to feel like I wasn't about getting his loot, so I waited until he picked an outfit and told me to try it on.

I went into the dressing room, and the damn dressing room even looked better than Rainbow's. I tried on the outfit, and the material felt way better than the $9.99 special I'd gotten from Rave. When I pulled up their logo capris, I fell in love with the way they fit my body. I put on the tank top and sandals and came out to let Dollar see me.

"That's hot. Keep that on," Dollar told me. I wasn't turning shit down; I looked too bossy. Dollar ordered the saleslady to give me one in every color and ring him up.

The tab went up to seventeen hundred dollars and I knew that was too much. "Dollar, that's way too much," I said. I didn't know what type of sexual act he wanted me to perform, spending that kind of money.

"I got it," he said as he pulled out seventeen crisp hundred-dollar bills.

The saleslady bagged my things up and sent me on my way. I couldn't believe Dollar had spent all that money on me. Shit, I only had ten outfits. I could have bought half the Rave with that money.

"Dollar, I want to say thank you. Really, you didn`t have to do that."

"I know," he said as he pulled me close. "But you my girl, and you can get whatever you want." Those words were like music to my ears. I wanted to be his girl.

After a few stops at the Coach store, Aldo's, and Express, Dollar and I grabbed a bite to eat and headed back to his place. When I walked in, my mouth dropped. I thought my grandma's house was nice, but Dollar had her beat. Dollar was moving some serious weight; you only saw shit like this on TV. I got excited to think that he called me his girl, that I could be laying up in here with him any time I wanted to.

Dollar's house complemented his life-style of balling outta control. His house decor was black and white like some gangster shit out of *Scarface*.

His butter-soft leather sectional was black with white throw pillows, and the acrylic glass table set the room off perfectly. Dollar had a 61-inch plasma TV hanging on the wall. His dining room had a huge black-and-white leather table with a thick glass top. The kitchen had Sub-Zero appliances and marble floors. Dollar's house represented money and lots of it. In Dollar's bedroom, he had the biggest bed you could find and another big-screen TV. it looked like something from MTV Cribs.

"You have a great house."

"Thank you. *Mi casa su casa,*" he said.

I took off my flip-flops before I climbed up on Dollar's bed. "This bed is huge," I gloated to Dollar.

I knew that with Dollar spending all that money on me, he was gonna want some pussy. I didn't mind giving it to him, either! I didn't know if I could satisfy Dollar; I'd never sucked a dick a day in my life, and the closest I got to seeing a dick was on Cinemax after ten o'clock. I was scared. I was still a virgin and I'd never even been touched by a boy. Dollar wasn't no boy — he was a man, and probably way too old for my sixteen-year-old pussy.

●●●●

Dollar stared Emerald down. She was beautiful and she had a hot body, but her movements told him that she was scared of him. He guessed that she was still a virgin, and he was glad. He reached out, rubbed her curly hair softly, and kissed her forehead. He felt her body trembling and knew she was nervous.

"If you don't want to, I can wait," he told Emerald, but he was hoping she wouldn't say no.

"I'm scared. I never had sex before."

"I won't hurt you," Dollar reassured Emerald. He pulled her newly purchased tank top over her head and tossed it on the floor. He kissed her softly on the lips and whispered to her, "I'm yours," then unhooked her bra and admired her nice, firm 36C breasts. He laid her down on the bed and began to lick her from head to toe. He sucked her breasts so softly that it sent Emerald into another world.

Dollar wasn't going to stop until he made Emerald cum, so he buried his head into her and she started shaking, screaming for him to stop. Dollar kept on licking her until he tasted her sweet juices and Emerald's body went numb.

Then Dollar undressed himself and released his big-ass dick he was packing under all those clothes. Emerald got nervous; she didn't know how all of that was gonna fit into her. When Dollar got closer, he saw the look of fear on Emerald's face. "I'ma take it slow, baby," he whispered as he slowly pushed his nine inches into her, inch by inch. Dollar was excited; Emerald's tight pussy felt good wrapped around his dick. "Tell me when I'm hurting you," he said.

Emerald just closed her eyes as tight as she could. It hurted like hell, but she knew he liked it because he was moaning her name the whole time. "Damn, baby, don't give my pussy away," Dollar moaned to Emerald. "Promise me you won't give it away?" he asked as he started to speed up.

Emerald felt every inch, every stroke of Dollar; she felt him in her stomach. "I won't!" she cried, trying to catch her breath.

It slipped Dollar's mind that he was pounding Emerald's virgin pussy like she'd been around the block. "Dollar, please, I can't take it!" Emerald cried.

When Dollar saw the tears in Emerald's eyes, he began to slow down. "I'm sorry, baby. You feel so good, baby." He started kissing Emerald's tears away, giving her slow, deep strokes. "Baby, you feel so good to me," he moaned in her ear.

Emerald just wanted it to be over. She thought this was the worst feeling she'd ever felt.

Dollar pulled himself off Emerald and went down to lick her pussy again. He buried his face in her and moaned, "Baby, this mine," while he was eating her out. Emerald liked this feeling. This feeling felt good to her.

Dollar finished licking her and then climbed back on top of her, pushing himself into her slowly. This time it didn't feel so bad. He stroked slowly, making each stroke deeper until his whole nine inches was inside her. Emerald could have sworn he was deep into her guts. Dollar looked into Emerald's eyes and kissed her on the lips; he began to work her slowly, but this time Emerald didn't push him away. It felt good to her. Emerald started rubbing his back and kissing Dollar's neck. He was stroking her the right way.

After another fifteen minutes, Dollar started to pound Emerald like no tomorrow was coming. "Emerald, baby, I'm cummin!" Emerald had no idea what he was talking about, but after two long deep strokes, Dollar pulled himself out and came on Emerald's stomach.

"Shit, girl, you gone make me marry you," he gasped.

Emerald laughed. She was kind of clueless about the whole sex world and didn't know if Dollar liked her. Dollar grabbed Emerald, pulled her close to him, and got under the covers. Emerald wanted Dollar to hold her with his big arms. They both fell asleep; Emerald felt safe with Dollar, and she was glad that he was hers.

They woke up about three hours later. Emerald looked at the clock and saw that it was eight o'clock. "Dollar, I have to go home," she said.

"Why?"

"Because my grandma gone kill me."

"You can move in with me," he said.

Emerald looked at Dollar. She knew he meant it, but her grandma would never go for that shit. "Look, Dollar, I would love to, but the truth is, I'm only sixteen and I know you're older than me. Trust me, I won't say anything, "cause I like you."

"I kind of figured that. It's cool." He reached into his nightstand and pulled out a house key. "Here's a key. Be careful and don't lose it."

Emerald was shocked. She couldn't believe it. "Are you sure?" she asked.

"Yeah. You my girl. Whatever I got, you got," Dollar said. "I got something for you." He got out of the bed, pulled out a Razr cell phone, and handed it to her. "Here, so I can get in contact with you."

Emerald was happy that she'd found somebody to take care of her. They jumped into the shower, and then Dollar dropped Emerald off at home.

••••

I tiptoed up the stairs to my room to hide my new clothes from my grandma. Sissy came in to get the scoop on Dollar.

"Girl, that boy bought you all of that?" Sissy yelled.

"Girl," I yelled as I jumped outta bed and closed my door, "yes he did!"

"What you had to do?"

"Nothing!"

"Right," Sissy said sarcastically.

"Don't be jealous. I'm his girlfriend."

"You just met him."

"So get outta my room with that dumb shit," I told her.

Sissy left and I put up my new clothes and purses. I knew I was going to be shutting down Gage Park tomorrow.

Chapter 3
LET THE HATERS HATE

I woke up thirty minutes early took a shower and lotion my body up good. I pulled out the brand-new BEBE outfit I got from Dollar, the matching flip-flops, and my new Coach bag. I knew all the bitches was gone be pissed, because I was looking too fly. I blow-dried my hair and flatironed it. I put my bus card, the keys to my man's place, and my cell phone in my purse. I knew I was gone be the illest bitch in school today. Ain't no bitch rocking BEBE.

When I stepped off the bus, everyone was staring at me. Shit, I knew I was a ghetto superstar. I went to my locker and met up with Me Me.

"Girl, where you get the fly outfit from?" she asked.

"My new man bought it," I said.

"That nigga we met Saturday?"

"Yup, I got one in every color."

"Get the fuck outta here!" Me Me exclaimed.

"I'm serious," I said. "I was with him all yesterday."

"Damn! I knew I should have talked to him."

I smiled at her. "Don't be jealous."

"Did you fuck him?" she asked.

I didn't want to tell her the truth, because it would seem like I was a ho. "Not yet, but I will."

"You better. He ain't gone be dropping paper and not getting no pussy."

"Right."

Me Me shut her locker. "So what you doing after school?"

"Nothing planned."

"Good, we can go kick it at the mall," she said.

At the end of the day, I checked my cell phone and saw that I'd missed five calls from Dollar. I called him back. "Hey, baby," I said.

"Why you ain't picking up your phone?" he asked in a nasty tone.

"I'm in school, and I have to leave it in my locker or they'll take it. I only come back to my locker twice a day."

"Well, you need to make sure you check your phone after every period," Dollar said.

"I'm sorry, baby. Don't be mad at me."

"I'm not mad. I want to see you. Can I pick you up from school?"

"Yeah," I said. "I'll be out in ten minutes."

I guess I must have whipped this pussy on him, cuz he was getting jealous already. I packed my things up to leave school and saw Me Me and dem coming to my locker.

"You ready?" Me Me asked me.

"For what?"

"To go to the mall! We waiting."

"Oh, yeah. Dollar called and asked me to come and spend some time with him, so I'ma need a rain check."

"Bitch, we been doing this for a minute, you gone let that nigga break our plans?" Alicia yelled.

"Yes I am," I said. "You gotta problem with that?"

"He just using your ass, anyway," she said.

"Jealousy is a sickness, you know our saying? Let the haters hate."

I walked off and left my friends hanging for the first time, but it wasn't going to be the last time. The way I see it, dem bitches was just jealous because I pinned down a true baller and they got wankstas. Friends or no friends, dem bitches ain't finna come between me and my bread. Fuck 'em. My nigga always gone come first.

Chapter 4
QUALITY TIME

For the next three months, I spent all my free time with Dollar. I went home and then to Dollar's house. I saw a lot less of my friends; matter of fact, we only saw each other at the mall and didn't speak on the phone. When my friends was popping their lips about Dollar, I was quick to tell dem bitches to stay outta mines. I didn't give a damn about what nobody said about my man. Dollar was my knight in shining armor; he spoiled me with the finer things in life, and those bitches was jealous. Before I knew it, I owned five Gucci bags, a closet full of the finest gear, and a brand-new whip.

I skipped doing my chores and stayed out with Dollar when he asked me to. I didn't care about what Grandma would think or gave a fuck either; I wanted to move in with Dollar.

The problem was, Grandma didn't approve of my relationship. She felt I was being disrespectful and staying out at all times of the night. I hated coming in her house because there were just too many rules. No matter what time I came in, she was always popping her gums about something. I told myself that if she got fresh with me today, I'ma let her ass know to fall back. I didn't give a damn. I didn't have to live there.

My grandma was a hater. She hated on Dollar cuz my ride was flyer than hers. She was always popping shit about him selling drugs that wasn't even her business. It was more than her fucked-up boyfriend did, sitting around collecting SSI checks. Dollar had been nothing but respectful to her since he met her. She was gone make me snap out on her if she kept on popping shit.

I took a deep breathe before I got outta my car, it was only ten o'clock, and I wasn't trying to hear shit from nobody. When I walked past I overheard Grandma's stank-ass boyfriend popping at the mouth. "Jean, that girl being too grown," he said.

That motherfucker has lost his last mind. He ain't none of my daddy. "You need to keep my name outta your snag-gletooth mouth," I told him. "You don't even live here."

"You might disrespect Jean, but you ain't gone disrespect me."

"Fuck you! I wish you would put your hands on me. I'll have my man come over here and kick your ass." All I had to do was make one phone call to Dollar, and him and his peoples would be here in a matter of minutes. He didn't know nothing about my gangster.

"Emerald," my grandma said.

"What?"

"Emerald, what's your problem?"

"Nothing," I retorted.

"Yes it is. Why you coming in my house this time of the night?"

"Well, I ain't got to live here," I said.

"Jean, you see how smart her mouth is?" Grandma's boyfriend yelled.

"What you gone do about it?" I yelled, cuz he didn't know shit about me.

"Let the bitch leave, Jean," he said. "She ain't doing nothing but raising up your blood pressure, lord knows she already got mine sky-high."

"Bitch? Who you calling a bitch? I'll stab your ass." This nigga was way sleep on me. I'd slice his damn mouth.

"Emerald, watch your mouth," Grandma said.

"My mouth? He just called me a bitch, and you tell me to watch my mouth?" My grandma had lost her last mind! She gone let this crackhead-ass nigga get off the chain wit me?

"You need to put a belt on her ass, Jean," he said.

"Please," I snapped. Wouldn't nobody raise a belt to me and live to tell about it.

"Emerald, you're smelling yourself too strong," Grandma told me. "If you're ready for the ride that boy gone give you, then go ahead and leave."

"I love the ride," I said. "I ride the hell outta it almost every day."

"Emerald, I will not tolerate you disrespecting my house. Since you want to be grown, then go, but know this: once you leave, ain't no coming back."

I couldn't run up the stairs fast enough to pack my shit up and move in with my man.

"Emerald, where you going?" Sissy asked.

"I'm getting up outta here. I'm moving in with Dollar."

"Emerald, you don't know much about this boy. How serious can you be? You're always acting so dumb. That boy is a drug dealer and you ain't the only piece of pussy he got."

"Shut up, bitch! You just jealous you ain't got him."

"Emerald, please," Sissy begged. "You don't hang out with none of your friends no more. That nigga got you gone in the head."

"I don't have time for little kid shit like y'all do."

"Well, trust me when I tell you, that nigga is playing you, and you stupid enough to let him."

"Bitch, what your ugly ass know about a man?" I yelled as I stepped into Sissy's face. "You ain't never had one and probably never will. You're skinny and not as half as pretty as me, so be easy, *bitch*!"

"Don't get into my face," Sissy yelled. "The truth hurts. And I don't have a man by choice. I ain't got to run behind no nigga; they run behind me."

"Please, don't nobody want your busted-ass pussy," I told her.

I took all that I could; I didn't care about the rest of my clothes, because I can get new ones. When I walked down the stairs, I looked at Grandma one good last time. I left without a hug, a goodbye, a thank-you, nothing; I bounced!

●●●●

I pushed my new Benz straight to Dollar's crib at full speed. I made a few calls to his cell phone and he didn't answer, but I didn't think nothing of it. I pulled into the parking lot of Dollar's complex and made my way up to Apartment 2C, happy that this would be my home sweet home now.

When I turned the key and opened the door, the sound of a woman screaming at the top of her lungs hit me. My heart started racing. The trail of clothes leading to the bedroom told me that he was fucking. I grabbed a knife from the kitchen and kicked in the door to his bedroom.

"Oh, Dollar," a familiar voice moaned.

"You like this dick?" Dollar moaned.

"Yes, Big Daddy, I love your big-ass—"

Before the girl could finish her sentence, I pulled her off Dollar's big dick and threw her down to the floor. Dollar fumbled for the light and was shocked to see me standing in front of him with a knife in my hand. When I looked down at the bitch, I saw a face I'd known since the first grade.

"Bitch, how could you?" I yelled as I pulled my best friend Me Me by the hair. With no more questions asked, I proceeded to kick Me Me's ass like she was a nigga on the street. My face turned red as I choked Me Me so hard she was gasping for air. "I'll kill you, bitch!" I screamed while holding my grip tight.

Dollar tried to get control of me, but I kept on swinging my knife at him. Me Me sat still, cold, and naked on the floor. "How could you?" I yelled at Dollar.

"I'm sorry, baby," Dollar said as he tried to reach in and comfort me.

I fell to the floor with tears in my eyes. What was I gonna do? I had just basically told my grandma to kiss my ass and left. There was no way I could show back up at Grandma's door after all the bullshit I'd just done. Anyway, I wasn't gonna leave Dollar and let that bitch have him. That bitch bet not ever show her face again or I'll kill her ass!

Dollar saw the pain in my eyes. He was hurt that he'd hurt me like that. Dollar bent down on his knees and hugged me tightly. He said he was sorry so many times that he sounded like a broken record.

Me Me picked up her clothes and left, and I never talked to dem hoes again.

Chapter 5
THE NEW ME

After Me Me crossed me, I didn't give a fuck about nothing. Bitches ain't shit but hoes and tricks: Too Short said it the best. I didn't return any of dem bitches phone calls. Hating bitches get Xed outta my book. I don't phony kick it. Motherfuckers want to be on my man's big-ass dick but I ain't having it. Bitches best to know I'd slice a bitch about my dick and put they ass six feet deep.

For the next two months, Dollar tried his best to make up to me for fucking my best friend. Since I knew that, I upgraded my Benz to a 745 sitting on dem things. My shoe game became official, and I never wore the same thing twice. I was the rawest bitch in the CHI; hoes knew who I was when I came through. I made all dem hating bitches fall back. I didn't hang with bitches no more. They couldn't be trusted.

Then Dollar introduced me to his best friend S.L.'s wife. When I first met Ginger, she was flawless. I thought I was the baddest bitch to do it, but when I met her, I saw that I needed to step my game up. Her walk was so serious it put me in a daze; it was like she was gliding while throwing her hips. She looked like Apollonia from Purple Rain. Her body was perfect from her fingernails to her smooth skin down to her pearly white teeth. Ginger was really the rawest bitch in the CHI. She made me feel ugly.

Ginger stared me up and down, like she smelled fear on me. She ran her fingers through my long hair and smelled it. I pulled back because I ain't wit that freaky shit. She looked at Dollar and smiled. "Another young bitch," she said, laughing.

I was pissed. I didn't care who she was; I'd fuck that bitch up. She'd better ask Dollar about me before she started popping at the mouth.

"She cool," Dollar said to Ginger.

She walked around me, peeping my body out. I was pissed and ready to go. Dis bitch was crazy.

"What's up, young pussy?" she said to me.

"Excuse me. My name is Emerald," I said, rolling my eyes because this bitch was getting on my last nerve.

"What you say, young pussy Emerald?"

I looked at Dollar and gave him my ready-to-go face. I was trying to be as respectful as I could, but I don't play tricks with these hoes and she was about to meet my backhand. "Dollar, could you take me back home?" I asked, trying to stay calm and not lose it.

"Me and S.L. about to make a run. You gotta sit here until I get back."

"What?" I asked as my face frowned up so hard it could have been confused with a knot. "I ain't gone be able to do it."

I guess Ginger got offended, because she snapped back, "Take her ass with you, because I ain't trying to babysit no young pussy."

That was my breaking point. "Look, Ginger, I've been nothing but nice and respectful to you since I stepped into your house, but I don't care how young you think I am. I'll put my young foot so far up your Apollonia-looking ass you'll be shitting Gucci for weeks."

Ginger looked at me again, this time with a smile on her face "I like this one, Dollar," she moaned to him. "I like a woman who can stand up for herself. Dem young bitches used to let me run all over them, but you stood up for yourself. I was hoping you would. But let's get this clear: don't ever raise your voice in my house again, understand?"

"As long as you be easy, I understand," I answered. She was lucky, cuz I was ready to draw blood. And the bitch looked better than me, so I would'a fucked her up really good to get my crown back.

●●●●

Ginger had a black skintight cami dress on. Her body was stacked but her ass was a little smaller than mine. She was cut in all the right places; I could tell that she worked out.

"So, young pussy, when you meet Dollar?" she asked me.

"Can you please call me Emerald?" I asked.

"Whatever."

"I met Dollar six months ago," I said.

"How old are you?"

"Sixteen and a half."

"Damn, you bitches coming younger every time!" She laughed.

Ginger clearly didn't give a fuck about what she said to people, and it was starting to piss me off. "Can you please watch your mouth?"

"Girl, dis my house, and I guess you don't have any friends. That's why your ass is here with me."

"Well, I had some friends, but I caught one of dem bitches riding my man's dick."

"Damn, you should have joined in with them."

This bitch is crazy for real. Dollar needs to hurry up and come and get me. Ginger sat there looking me up and down; she had her legs crossed and it was making me uncomfortable.

"You want a drink, *Emerald*?" she asked me, smiling.

Now she trying to be funny. My nerves are wearing thin wit her ass. "Yeah, a drink would be cool."

Ginger threw her legs open and I caught a glimpse of her pussy. It was shaved bald. She walked to the bar, pulled out a bottle of Grey Goose, and poured me a glass. When she handed it to me, I was kind of scared; I had never taken a real drink before, and she sensed it. "Damn, young pussy, it's just a drink."

"Why are you so rude?" I asked her, because I was getting tired of her bullshit.

"I ain't rude. I just keep it real, and since I like you, I'ma hook your ass to some game."

"I'm listening," I said.

"You a young bitch with some young pussy. What, you trying to get this nigga to marry you?"

"Yeah."

"Well, first off, you need to stop dressing like a fucking teenybopper. You trying to be grown, so dress like a grown woman."

I was pissed. That bitch had some nerve. I was looking fly in my new Baby Phat outfit. "What's the matter with what I got on?"

"Nothing, if you sixteen, but a grown-ass woman ain't rocking no Air Ones. We rock stilettos." I wasn't the best heel wearer, and I swear I was hurting dem bitches with my fresh Air Ones. "Your hair is fucked up," Ginger went on. "Don't nobody but young bitches wear twists in their hair."

I was feeling real shitty. Here I was, walking around like I'm the baddest bitch who did it, and she done shut me down. "So what I gotta do?" I asked her, because I wanted to know. I wanted to be Dollar's wifey.

"First, take that bullshit off."

"What, my clothes?"

"What else? Stop asking dumb-ass questions."

I stood up feeling weird. I'd never gotten undressed in front of a woman. I took off my clothes and stood there in front of her in my panties and bra. When I revealed myself, she started busting up laughing, dis bitch was on my left nerve. I'ma put my backhand to dis ho in a minute. My body is the coldest!

"You are a young bitch," Ginger laughed. "Why you got on them grandma panties?"

"These are Victoria's Secret," I said.

"So? Grown women don't wear them kind of panties. Show a nigga some ass, you got a nice one."

I began to tremble as she ran her hand across the arch of my back. She went into her room and brought out a slinky Gucci dress and a pair of heels. Then she handed me a new thong and told me to put it on. I had to admit, I did look older and feel sexier. Ginger pulled my hair down outta my twist and brushed it back, then finished me off with a MAC makeover. I walked to the mirror and admired myself. I did feel grown.

"Now, young pussy, you need to shave your pussy hair," she said.

"What?" I yelled. I wasn't shaving my pussy in front of her.

"Shave your pussy bald! Don't nobody want a mouthful of hair."

"I'll do it later," I said.

"Of course. You know what to use?"

"A razor?" I replied. Her loud laughter told me I wasn't right.

"A razor, girl? You gonna have bumps for days!" She chuckled as she got off the bed and walked into the oversized bathroom. "Use this Nair, but be very careful. If you use it wrong, your pussy will be on fire."

"Well, how am I supposed to use it?"

"Damn, you young bitches ain't good for nothing! Take off your panties," she told me.

I hesitated at first. The bitch was OC, but since I was on my third glass of Grey Goose, I was feeling kind of loose. I pulled off the dress and panties and stood there in just my bra.

She laid me down on the bed and told me to push my legs back, she put a thick cotton strips in the crack of my pussy and told me to hold it. The Nair was cold when she rubbed it on me. She put Nair around the top of my pussy, my lips, and the crack of my ass, then got up and told me to lie there for five minutes. I didn't feel a tingle or nothing, so I didn't know if the stuff was working.

Ginger came back five minutes later with another drink. She took a warm towel and started wiping away the Nair. Before I knew it, I had no hair; my pussy was as smooth as a baby's ass.

I got undressed, got into the shower, and washed myself up as I gulped down the drink she gave me. Once I got out of the shower and dried off, I felt kind of funny, like the room was spinning. When I got back into the room, Ginger was lying on her bed waiting for me. "I feel funny," I told her as I laid down next to her.

"It's okay," she said. "I'ma take care of you."

Before I knew it, Ginger had my towel off and her face between my legs. I couldn't fight her; I was gone, and besides, she was licking my pussy so good I didn't want her to stop. "Ginger, what are you doing to me?" I asked.

"Tasting me some young pussy."

Ginger licked me from my pussy to my ass crack and back again. She was licking me so good, I never tried to make her stop. "You like this, young pussy?"

"Yeah," I moaned, because I did. I loved it. She knew all the right places to lick and suck. She was much better at this than Dollar. "Oh, Ginger, I'm about to cum."

Ginger stuck her tongue in my pussy and started to fuck me with it. I hadn't noticed her tongue was that long. Before I knew it, I busted so hard.

I looked down at Ginger and she was down there still licking.

She licked up all my juices, then got up, pulled out the biggest dildo I'd ever seen, and fucked me with it until I begged her to stop. Once she finished me, I was numb and turned out.

Chapter 6
BABY ON BOARD

When I woke up this morning, my stomach was cramping and I hadn't had a period in three months. I kept fooling myself about not being pregnant, but I finally went to the drugstore and bought a test.

I peed on the stick. The directions said to wait three minutes and if the stick turned pink, I was pregnant. As soon as I peed, the stick turned pink! I was happy that I was going to be Dollar's baby momma.

I jumped into bed with Dollar and showed him the stick.

"What's that?" Dollar asked.

"I'm pregnant! We're pregnant!"

"What?"

"Yes! Are you happy?"

Dollar just looked at me. He didn't seem too happy, but I knew he would come around sooner or later. "Go to the doctor and find out how many months you are," he told me.

The next day, I went to the Planned Parenthood clinic and found out I was three and a half months pregnant. When I told Dollar, he still didn't seem happy; he just brushed me off.

"Dollar, ain't you happy we having a baby?" I asked.

"Not really."

"Why not?"

"Because I didn't want kids, Emerald."

When he said that, my heart sank. If he didn't want the baby, that meant he wasn't gonna love the baby. "You want me to get a abortion?"

"We'll see next month when you have a ultrasound."

I didn't know what in the hell that had to do with the price of tea in China. But I didn't like to stress Dollar out, so if he said wait until next month, I would wait.

●●●●

When I laid back on the table and the doctor put that cold gel on my stomach, I got scared. Then he pressed the wand against my belly and started moving it around, and I saw my baby for the first time. I saw my baby's head, feet, arms and fingers. I was happy to see my baby alive inside of me.

Dollar, on the other head, kept demanding the doctor to tell him the sex of the baby.

"I'm trying to find out, sir," the doctor said. Then he put the wand in the right position and said the magic words. "It's a girl."

"What?" Dollar yelled. "Are you sure?"

The doctor took a picture and showed Dollar that it was a girl. Dollar got up all pissed off and walked out of the room.

I got dressed and ran out after him. I didn't understand why he was so mad. "Dollar, what's the matter?"

"Nothing. You getting a abortion."

"What?" I gasped.

"Tomorrow."

"Why?"

"I don't want no silly-ass little girl," he said. "I spoke, and I don't want to hear nothing else about it."

That day, for the first time, I hated Dollar. What did he mean, silly-ass little girl? That night I cried myself to sleep. I knew that in the morning, I would no longer have a baby.

When we made to the clinic, the nurse checked me in and took me to the back. I told Dollar to pay for me to be put to sleep, because I couldn't bear to be awake and watch my baby get killed. It was a two-day procedure because I was so far along. The first night it hurt like hell when I had all those sticks up in me. I cried all night long because of the pain and the thought of hurting my baby.

The next day, I returned and laid down on the table, the doctor put me to sleep, and when I woke up, I didn't have a baby no more. I left that clinic with half of my heart missing. I didn't speak to

Dollar for the whole ride home, and that night, I laid awake thinking about my lost child.

Chapter 7
AFTERMATH

Dollar did everything he could to make up for the abortion of our child. After I talked to Ginger about it, I knew I wasn't ready to be nobody's momma anyway, so I thanked Dollar for making that smart choice. I wasn't gonna be tied down in the house with a baby.

My seventeenth birthday was coming and I wanted to have some fun. I needed to put the things Ginger schooled me to in motion, so I officially stepped my game up. I only rocked six-inch stilettos, True Religion jeans, and wifebeaters, and that was my off day. I got my hair done twice a week and hurt the mall regularly.

Dollar wanted to me to get some businesses in my name to clean up some of his money, so I opened a boutique on the west side of Chicago called Icey. I also purchased three apartment buildings. Dollar was big-time. He had all the right people lined in his pockets, so it didn't matter that I was underage; money talked and bullshit walked. Dollar was able to put it all in my name, and I didn't mind; if he ever went to jail, I'd still have all that property.

My boutique was clocking in mad paper. I started to design my own line of T-shirts with the Icey logo and got mad paid. That was my own money that I kept from Dollar, and he didn't know anything about it. My taste in clothes was excellent, and I even branched off into making jeans. I was the ghetto Kimora Lee Simmons, getting all the loot.

I told Dollar that I wanted a Bentley GT for my birthday and he paid me no nevermind. He was acting like my birthday didn't matter, popping his mouth about all he did during the year. I wasn't trying to hear that shit.

With Ginger's guidance, I'd learned how to suck a mean dick: I mean the kind that makes a man's legs shake. I was raw. I let Ginger eat my pussy two to three times a week. Dollar didn't know that Ginger turned me out like that. I loved getting my pussy ate by a bitch. I don't consider myself to be gay; I just let Ginger break me off from time to time. I mean, if you let her lick you one time, you'd be running back too. The bitch is talented.

Ginger had turned me out so bad that Dollar poured me even more money. I fucked him good every night, and when my period was on, I'd suck the life outta his dick. I never gave Dollar no lip. Ginger schooled me to the rules of dating a street nigga, and the first rule was not to stress him out. So no matter how many bitches popped shit about him, I never questioned him. All my man got when he came home was a home-cooked meal, a good dick suck, and a backrub. I swear, every morning I had at least five hundred dollars laid on the nightstand.

I never complained to Dollar. I had no reason to; even though he couldn't eat pussy like Ginger, his fuck game was strong and he knew how to beat the pussy up good. My regular visits to Ginger satisfied my other cravings.

●●●●

I closed the shop up early today so I can pick up the rent money and make it home. I made sure I was always there before Dollar came in so I could have his food ready. I was cooking his favorite today — fried pork chops and candied yams — so I could butter him up about my car.

When Dollar came in the house, he slammed the door, which told me he was pissed off. He only slam's the door when he's pissed off.

I greeted him with a kiss. "Hey, babe, I made your favorite."

"I'm not hungry!" he snapped at me.

"Tell Momma what's wrong," I purred as I removed his coat and pushed him down on the couch.

"I'm just sick of this bullshit."

"What, hustling?"

"Yeah, everything," Dollar said. "I don't have too many people I can trust."

Dollar was big in the streets. He was the Don, so he had a lot of stress on him. Dollar was a teddy bear wit me, but with a nigga on the streets, he was a barracuda. Everybody knew Dollar meant business. I'd seen him slap a few niggas about coming up short with his money, and if you crossed him, you would be made a example of on the Channel 5, 7, and 9 news. Dollar only trusted a few people, and in the dope game, that was too many. So I understood when he was stressed out. He had a business to run. He was the leader, and he always had to be on his A game at all times.

"Well, you can trust me, Big Daddy," I whispered to him as I unbuckled his pants to release some of his tension. That's one thing about a powerful dick suck: it can make the hardest man soft in a matter of minutes. I knew how to relax his mind and take the stress of the world off his shoulders. I'm tha rawest bitch in the game and he knows that; that's why he keeps me laced, cuz I get him right every time. When Dollar's stressed out like this, I get on my knees because that makes him feel superior. I pushed Dollar deep into my throat, bobbing my head like no tomorrow was coming.

"Damn, Emerald, you know how to make a nigga feel good," he moaned.

Damn right I do. I'm the coldest bitch. Shit, if they was giving out awards for the best dick-sucker, I'd win best of all time. Im tha rawest! I wanted my man to feel good at home because it's a place of peace for us. Dollar never had to worry about coming home and getting mistreated; he knew I had his back. I slurped down his cum like pancake syrup, and once I released him, Dollar fell back trying to catch his breath. "Baby, you know you treat me too good."

"I know, sweetheart."

"I need you to do me a favor," he said.

"Anything, Dollar."

"Okay. I wouldn't normally ask you nothing like this, but I'm in a bind."

"Go ahead," I said.

"I need you to make a run."

"A run?"

"Yeah. I need you to go drop something off in Michigan."

"What?"

"You know what, Emerald. Don't act slow."

I couldn't believe dis nigga done asked me to drop off some dope like he was crazy. How could he? If he loved me, he wouldn't want me to risk myself. "Dollar, I don't know. I ain't trying to go to jail."

"You ain't gone get caught," he said. "I thought you said you'd do anything for me. I guess you lied to me."

"Dollar, that's not true. You know I would, but I don't want to go to jail for nobody."

"Not even me?" He looked at me with sad eyes. I just looked at him, not knowing what to say. My body was frozen, and he could tell by my body language that I was saying "Nigga, hell naw."

Dollar got up and walked away from me with his sad puppy-dog eyes. I felt terrible. Dollar has been taking care of me since I was sixteen; he took me from nothing and gave me something. He never asked me to do nothing. How could I be so selfish to the only man who ever loved me or gave me anything?

I walked into our bedroom and knelt down in front of Dollar. I wanted to show him how much I loved him. I took his hand and placed it on my face. I wanted him to feel the love that was there for him. "Dollar, you're the only man that gave a damn about me. I'll do anything for you. If you want me to make the run, I will."

Dollar knelt down next to me and kissed me softly on the lips. "Look, I love you, Emerald. None of this shit matters to me but you. I would never put you into a position that would hurt you. It would only be this one time, and I have a surprise waiting on you for your birthday."

I was excited and scared at the same time. I knew I needed to trust Dollar fully. That night, I just wanted him to hold me close so I could let myself go and trust him all the way.

Chapter 8
THE RUN

My stomach was cramping bad when I woke up, even though my period wasn't due for another two weeks I felt like I was coming on. I saw Big Momma's number on my caller ID. I hadn't heard from her in a while. "Good morning, Big Momma," I said.

"Happy birthday, baby."

"Thank you."

"So, you got plans?"

"No, nothing."

"Well, you can come by," she said. "I made you your favorite jelly cake. We miss you."

"Thanks, Big Momma."

"So, you get yourself back into school?"

"Big Momma, please don't start with me," I said. "I own a clothing store and I'm doing very well."

"I'm just saying you can go a little far with a education, that's all."

"Um hm," I said because I really didn't want to hear that noise she was popping. "Where Sissy?"

"She right here, baby."

Sissy came on the phone. "What up, bitch?"

"Sissy, watch your mouth around Big Momma! Did you get the clothes I sent you?"

"Yeah, thank you."

"Good. You know, I paid your school up until the end of the year, so you should be all good."

"I know, Emerald," she said. "Can we hang out this weekend?"

"Yeah, but don't be fucking up in school. Big Momma told me some boy done got into your head. You make sure you finish school."

"Unlike you, I ain't no dropout," Sissy retorted.

"Well, don't be. I'll see you tomorrow. We can go out with Ginger."

"That bitch is a dyke," Sissy said.

"No, she ain't."

"Well, she be looking at me all funny, like she wanna eat me or something."

"Bye, Sissy." As I put the phone down, I couldn't stop laughing because she was right— Ginger can eat the hell outta some pussy.

I got dressed in my Juicy track suit and went into the front, where Dollar had all this dope lying on the table. My heart started racing. "This is what you want me to drop off?" I asked. There was enough dope there to send me away for a long time.

"Emerald, damn! Stop acting like a little-ass girl!" Dollar shouted. "Now you gonna drop that shit off like you promised."

I stared at him. He'd never yelled at me before. I put my shoes on, got the directions, and put the dope in the trunk of my car. My hands were sweating. It was gonna be a five-hour ride there and back. I looked at Dollar and I was scared. It was like all that mattered to him was getting that dope there. I brushed by him without saying nothing.

Once I jumped behind the wheel, the situation became more serious.

"Emerald!" Dollar yelled my name to snap me outta my daze. I looked up at him like a lost child. "Don't speed, wear your seatbelt, and if you can, don't stop. Call me when you get there."

I pulled off into the sunset, headed down Highway 90/94 to Michigan. I put my Beyonce CD in to calm my nerves. When I passed by my first state trooper, I could'a pissed on myself, but after the third hour, I was more ready to get there. It seemed like forever.

When I finally arrived in Detroit, I didn't relax; I still had a trunk full of dope to drop off. I made my way to where Dollar wanted me to go and pulled into the garage that was open for me. Once I cut the engine off, I exhaled.

A tall light-skinned guy with pretty gray eyes came out, stared me up and down, and frisked me. It was like he got free feels off me as his big hands went up and down my body.

"Open the trunk," he said to me.

I opened the trunk and handed him the two bags of dope. After searching through the bags, he handed me two bags full of money. "It's all there," he said. I didn't care; I just wanted to get home safely. I took the money, tossed it into the trunk, and drove away.

I stopped at the local gas station for something to drink, then headed back to Chicago. I called Dollar and told him that the drop was done and I'd see him at home.

I'd never been more happy to be home. When I walked in, Dollar was nowhere to be found. I put the bags of money in his walk-in closet. My bed had never looked so good, but there was a note from Dollar telling me to meet him down at this club called Dreams that he was wanting to buy.

I didn't want to leave the house. I'd made it across state lines with enough dope to put me away for life, and now I wanted to sleep and not be bothered with anybody. But Dollar said meet him, so I had to meet him. In my closet, there was a new Gucci dress hanging up with shoes to match. It made me feel a little better that Dollar had gone outta his way to buy me something new.

I jumped into the shower, lotioned myself up, and sprayed on my Be Delicious because it smelled the best. After I made myself up, I felt good again. I don't know why I'm tripping. That drop is done and I'll never have to do it again.

●●●●

When I pulled up in front of Dreams, the place looked dead. I didn't know why Dollar wanted to buy it. When I entered the club, the lady at the front desk told me Dollar was waiting for me downstairs.

The place looked empty. I flicked the light on and everybody jumped outta nowhere yelling "Surprise!" I was shocked. It was packed: everybody I knew was there.

Sissy ran up to me, hugging me and saying, "Happy birthday!" I was surprised at how much Sissy had filled out; she had hips and ass. She still dressed old lady, but she looked just like me.

Ginger was looking sexy. I was definitely rolling through to see her tomorrow so she can give me a happy birthday lick.

I went to find Dollar to give him a kiss for throwing me a party. It was the first party I'd ever had. Dollar was sitting at the table talking to S.L., and he was looking too sexy. I went and gave him a big hug and a kiss. "Thank you, baby, you surprised me!"

"Anything for you, Emerald."

"Wow, how'd you plan this party without me knowing?" I asked.

"Sissy helped me."

"You're the best man ever," I gloated as I sat down into his lap. Dollar smelled good and looked good. He was turning me on. I whispered in his ear, "I'ma thank you real good tonight."

Then I got up and clucked my Gucci heels around the party. I looked around the room to see who I recognized. Most of the bitches in there I didn't know at all. I went over to shoot the shit with Ginger. "What's up, Ginger?"

"Nothing. You like your party?"

"Yeah, I was surprised."

"Me and S.L. going to Mexico tomorrow. You should tell Dollar to come with us."

"How we gone get some tickets?"

"My cousin works for the airline," Ginger said. "She can get them."

"Cool, I'll go and tell him."

I walked back over to Dollar and looked at him, I'm the luckiest girl in the world. I have a balling man who really loves me: who could ask for more? I mean, he'd gone outta his way to plan this whole party for me. I leaned over and gave him another kiss. "Dollar, baby, I love you."

"I love you too, Emerald."

"I put the money in your closet because I didn't know where else to put it," I whispered.

"Cool," he said. "What you think about the place?"

"I guess it's cool."

"I need you to come down and sign the papers for it."

"This is in my name too?"

"Yeah. Is there a problem?" Dollar asked.

"No problem. I just wonder if they gonna say something about me, having all these stuff and only seventeen."

"White people do it all the time. Stop worrying, daddy gone take care of you."

"Good, because I want to go to Mexico tomorrow with S.L. and Ginger," I said.

"Cool. Anything you want, you got."

I hugged Dollar, because he was right. He has been giving me nothing but the best of everything since I met him. I never wanted for nothing. Any bitch would die to have property like me. I'm worth a lot of ends. Dollar always looked out for me. He could'a put all that stuff in his momma's name, but he trusted me with it. Shit, what's to complain about? I'm tha most wanted bitch in the CHI. Everybody wants to be me!

I danced for hours until the DJ called it a night. Then I grabbed Dollar. I couldn't stop smiling. I was so happy on the inside that nothing could top this off.

"I got another surprise for you," Dollar said to me.

"What?"

"Close your eyes," he said, and I did. I followed him to the front of the club and waited for him to give me my cue. "Open them, baby."

When I opened my eyes, there was my baby, a brand new black Bentley GT. I screamed as loud as I could. "Baby, you got it for me!" I jumped into his arms.

"I told you, Emerald, you'll never have to ask me anything twice."

Boy, I'ma be the rawest bitch in the CHI. I'm shutting these hoes down with this one. I jumped behind the wheel and imagined myself flossin', pulling up to my store. "Give me the keys!" I yelled to Dollar. I wanted to take my ride for a new spin. "Come on, Sissy," I said. Sissy got in and we went and bent tha blocks.

"Boy, I love Dollar," I told Sissy.

"You and everybody else."

"What?"

"Emerald, I hope you don't think he being faithful to you."

"I don't give a fuck about a bitch. They ain't getting it like I'm getting it."

"Why you playing yourself?" she asked.

"Sissy, I didn't bring you along to be hating on me," I said. "I don't give a fuck what you or nobody else thinks. Everybody can kiss my ass."

"Just be careful."

It was time for me to drop Sissy's hating ass off. I ain't got time for dem bitches to be popping their lips about my man. Fuck 'em. Fuck everybody who got something to say. Jealousy is a sickness, and even though she my sister, I'll make her ass walk home if she keep disrespecting my gangster.

I tried to rush back to Big Momma's house so I could drop Sissy's loudmouth ass off. Bitches quick to pop shit about Dollar, but they just want me to leave him so they can take the top spot. I ain't having it.

I stopped and told her to get out. "See you later, Sissy." I couldn't pull off fast enough. Sissy was just a young ho that didn't know no better.

When I made it home, I jumped in the shower, then got in the bed with Dollar and showed him how much I thanked him for my new ride.

Chapter 9
MEXICO

We woke up early to catch the flight to Mexico. Them bastards got the airport all fucked up: you have to get there two hours early and shit. I packed light, since we was only staying there for the weekend. I packed one suitcase and a carry-on bag with my panties and bras and toiletries.

I woke Dollar up five times and he still wouldn't budge. He yelled for me to make him some breakfast. I made him a bacon, egg, and cheese sandwich, then put our bags by the door and waited for Dollar. I paced tha floor waiting for him, this was my first time on an airplane and I was excited.

"Come on, baby, let's go," I said anxiously.

"Damn, Emerald, can a nigga pee? I don't like to pee on them planes."

Once we made it to the airport, we met up with Ginger and S.L. I was so excited about going to Mexico for the first time. We checked our luggage and made our way to the checkpoint. Me and Ginger both had carry-on bags, so we placed them on the rolling table and walked down toward the screening monitors. Ginger had on a skimpy shirt with no bra; I was surprised that S.L. let her up outta the house with that on. When our bags made it to the checkpoints, Ginger tripped and her boobs popped outta her shirt.

The guards all ran to her rescue looking at Ginger's firm round breasts. "You need some help, ma'am?"

Ginger squeezed her breasts, pinched her nipples, and pulled her shirt back up. "I got it, sweetie, thank you."

We grabbed our bags and went to the gate. I looked out the window in a daze, wondering what my life would'a been like if I'd never met Dollar.

"You happy, baby?" Dollar asked.

"I'm past happy, baby. I love you."

"Good. You know I'll do anything for you," he said.

"Yeah, and I'll do the same for you."

When it was time to board the plane, we all were in first class. The seats were so plush and big. We was gonna be on the plane for seven hours.

When the plane took off, it scared me; the turbulence was making the plane shake. The higher we got, the more my ears started to hurt. "Dollar, my ears hurt, baby."

"Just hold my hand," he said. "We'll be up in the air in a minute."

I grabbed Dollar's hand tight until the plane leveled itself out. Once we got all the way in the air, the plane rode smooth and I began to calm down. All that shit made me sleepy, so I closed my eyes and got some shut-eye.

"Please fasten your seatbelts," the pilot said.

I figured we was going to land, so I snapped my seatbelt on, hoping the landing would be better than the take-off. Once we made it to the ground safely, I said thank you to the Lord. We got our luggage and headed for the hotel.

The hotel was beautiful; this was a perfect way to top off my birthday weekend. Dollar got our keys and we went up to the room. Dollar had gotten us a villa with a upstairs and a downstairs. The room was off the chain: the bed was two times the size of a normal bed. We was going to do some serious fucking up in here.

Dollar told me he was leaving to go to see S.L.'s room. I wanted to unpack and unwind, and I needed to take a shower because we had a long ride in.

I unpacked my suitcase and put all my clothes in the drawer. Then I went and got my carry-on bag, and it was heavy. Shit, I didn't remember putting that much shit in my bag. I unzipped my bag and poured out all my stuff on the bed. There was something wrapped up in my clothes. I unwrapped my clothes and found three kilos of dope in my carry-on bag. That's why my bag was heavy — Dollar had put this dope in my bag.

I was pissed. What if them people had found this dope? I would'a gone to jail. Dollar has gone too far.

I ran down to Ginger's villa, ringing the doorbell like I was crazy.

She opened the door. "Damn, bitch, what's your problem? I heard you the first time."

"Where's Dollar?" I yelled I was so pissed off, my face was turning red.

"He left. They went somewhere. What's the matter with you?"

"That nigga put three kilos of dope in my bag and he didn't say nothing to me."

"Did you get caught?" Ginger asked.

"What does that have to do with anything?"

"Look, Emerald, you're dating a drug dealer. You trying to play a grown woman's game. If you too scared for this shit, then let that nigga know, because he don't need no little-ass girl."

"Did you know?" I asked.

"Yeah. Why you think I popped out my tits?"

I looked at Ginger I could'a slapped her ass. "I don't like nobody playing with my life."

"Look, Emerald, didn't that nigga just cop you a Bently, threw you a party, flew you out here first class? Shit, that cost money. You hurting the mall regularly ,right?"

"Yeah, but—"

"But nothing. Shit, if you can spend that nigga money, you can help him make it. And if you ain't gone be all the way down for that nigga, than let him know so he can find him a ride-or-die chick."

"I am down for him," I said.

"Well, then, stop being a scaredy-cat."

"I just wish he would have told me."

"Then let that nigga know that, but we came down here to have fun."

"Yeah," I said as I walked off back to my room. I knew Ginger was right. I just wished Dollar had told me so I could have been prepared, that's all.

When I got back to the room, Dollar was standing there drinking some juice like nothing happened.

"Hey, I was looking for you," he said.

"Was you? cuz I was looking for you."

"What up, boo?"

"Don't boo me," I said. "Why you ain't tell me you put all that dope in my bag?"

"Because I didn't want you acting all scared."

"What if I got caught?"

"I knew Ginger was gone handle it."

"That shit ain't cool, Dollar."

"Look, it's over and done with," he said.

I just looked at him. I hated to stress Dollar out, especially when he'd been so good to me.

"Let's get in the shower," he said. "I need to get my dick sucked."

"Nah, I'm cool."

Dollar took two steps back and looked at me in disbelief. "You cool."

"Um hum."

Dollar jumped into the shower, then walked out and slammed the door. I just laughed. That's what his ass get trying to play me, so I got the last laugh on his ass.

After it got late and Dollar had been gone for a while, I felt bad. I thought about what I'd done to my man, and I wanted to make it up to him. I lit some candles around the bedroom soaked in my Carol's Daughter Mango Mélange bubble bath, lotioned my skin and put on my lace cami nightie, then laid down on the bed and waited for Dollar to come back.

I drifted off to sleep. The sounds of the leaves hitting the window woke me up. I looked at the clock and it was eleven o'clock at night. Dollar hadn't stepped a foot back into our room since he left.

I got my robe, put my flip-flops on, and went down to the beach to see if I could find Dollar. I had walked nearly a mile when I reached a cabana with moans coming from it. I went in and found Dollar getting head from a Puerto Rican chick.

I snatched that bitch by her hair while she still had Dollar's dick in her mouth. I guess she must have bit him, because he was hollering. "Bitch, you must don't know what I do to bitches about my dick," I yelled. I slapped that bitch with my backhand and that bitch got up and took off running.

"So that's what we on now?" I asked Dollar.

"Shit, I asked you to suck it and you said no."

"Please."

"Shit, I think my dick bleeding," he said.

"That's what you get." I couldn't stop laughing at Dollar crying like a baby. When we made it back to the room, I wrapped a cold towel around his dick.

"Emerald, I'm sorry, baby. You did all this for your man."

"I did. Don't let it happen again."

Dollar's dick was so sore that we didn't fuck that night. The next day, Dollar and S.L. went to handle some business—I guess they had to drop off the dope I smuggled over here. Later that evening, after me and Ginger went on a serious shopping spree, we got with the guys and went jet skiing, scuba diving, and parasailing. I had so much fun. I felt like my life couldn't get any better; nobody could break me and Dollar apart.

The next day, Dollar rented a yacht for me and him to spend some time alone. When I got on, he had a little picnic set up for us. I was surprised; sometimes Dollar can be so romantic. I laid back and let Dollar feed me strawberries dipped in whipped cream. I'm so happy to be in Dollar's world. I really loved him.

Dollar took the whipped cream and rubbed it all over my body. He licked every inch of me from the bottom of my feet all the way up to the top of my head. Dollar was a beast in the bed. Shit, how perfect could you have it? Good sex, money, power, and respect. Shit, being Dollar's bitch was the best thing that ever happened to me. I know he cheats on me; that comes along with the streets, but I'll be damned if I let a bitch take my spot.

On our last night in Mexico, we took a long walk on the beach and made love right there on the soft sand. That moment was magical. On the way back home, I joined the Mile-High Club and we got it on for hours on the plane. I showed Dollar why I was da baddest bitch.

Chapter 10
SISSY

I got a call from Big Momma about Sissy again; she said she'd been staying out late. I told Big Momma, "Don't worry about Sissy, cuz I'ma handle her ass." She had me fucked up, thinking I was dropping all this bread for school and she out there wildin' out.

I told Sissy I was picking her up so we could go shopping and spend some time together. We hadn't done that in a while, and I needed to talk some sense into her. She at least needed to tell me what she finna do. I wasn't dropping bread on UIC if she wasn't finishing her degree.

"What's up?" I asked Sissy as she stepped out of the house in an Icey jogging suit, looking too pretty. It amazed me how much we looked alike. The shit was actually scary. People even mixed us up cuz we looked like twins.

"I want to drive my car," Sissy said to me.

"Fine." I jumped outta my ride and got into Sissy's brand-new CLK, courtesy of me. I bought Sissy that ride cuz she finished high school early and I was very proud of her. She was really smart. I didn't want her chasing paper—I wanted her to finish school. I kept her laced so she didn't have to run behind no niggas.

It was hard for me to swallow her messing up and shit. She didn't need to be hanging out. Of course, she needed to get fucked—I understood that, I wasn't trying to fuck up her action. But she'd never have to run up behind no nigga. Whatever she needed, she didn't have to ask me twice; I'd make sure she got it.

Sissy threw in her Lil' Kim CD and pulled off. She was bumping "Shut Up Bitch" loud as hell. I reached in and turned down the radio cuz I needed to talk to her.

"Bitch, don't touch my shit!" she said. "Do I jump into yo' car turning down your radio?"

"Sissy, you better watch yo' fucking mouth. I can touch anything I want to in this motherfucker. I paid for it."

"You ain't paid for nothing. Actually, you used Dollar's money, so he paid for it."

I looked at Sissy. "Bitch!" I yelled, almost slapping the shit out of her. I had to catch myself. She was lucky she was driving, or she would have been slapped. "Bitch, Dollar ain't paid for shit. I bought you this with my own ends."

Sissy looked at me, smacked her lips, and rolled her eyes. "You ain't got no money." She smirked.

I looked at her and wanted to choke her ass for flipping off at the mouth about shit she didn't know about. "You don't know what the fuck I got, bitch," I said.

"Right," Sissy said.

Sissy always think she better than somebody cuz she in college. She ain't know shit about me. I got a fat-ass bank account. I don't need Dollar's ends. If I whip out my bank statement on her ass, she'll be kissing my ass, I thought. I didn't give a fuck about Sissy talking shit, but if she didn't shut her fucking mouth, she'd be going to a junior college instead of a university. I didn't have to put her through school. *She lucky I love her ass, or she'll be going to Malcolm X College instead of U.I.C, so she better watch her step.*

"I'm putting you through school, so don't you ever forget that shit," I said.

"Where we going?" she asked, ignoring me.

"What's yo' deal? Some nigga done got into yo' head that tuff?"

"Please, Emerald, do I look like you?"

"Well, actually, you do," I said. "We look like twins, smartass."

"You know what I mean," she said. "I ain't letting these niggas get in my head. I'm smarter than that."

I didn't know if that was a low blow from Sissy or what, but she was getting on my left nerve. "Well, you acting like it, and I ain't got no fucking money to waste! That school hitting my pockets hard, so I think you better straighten up and fly right around this bitch."

"You ain't none of my mommy!"

"Bitch, I am yo' mommy, and you keep getting smart with me, I'ma slap yo' ass in the mouth."

"Please." Sissy laughed as she rolled her eyes.

"So, who is he?" I asked.

"Who?"

"That nigga you messing with. I think I need Dollar to pay him a visit."

"Girl, ain't nobody scared of Dollar's stank ass," she said.

"Don't disrespect my man!"

"Girl, he ain't all yo' man! You share him."

That was my final straw with Sissy. She knew I didn't give a fuck about that hating shit she be pulling. "You worry about your own nigga and I'll worry about mine, cuz I don't give a fuck about yo' opinion about my man. I'm number one to him and them hoes is just pussy, so I don't give a fuck. He ain't leaving me for none of their asses, so he can fuck. I don't care."

"Do you have any self-respect? You letting that nigga play you like a game of dominoes."

Now I saw why I didn't hang around Sissy that much. She was just a young ho, always talking shit. "Sissy, I didn't ask to go out and have yo' mouth overloading yo' ass."

"Whatever, Emerald, and I don't need you try'na be my momma, neither. I ain't no dummy. I'm gonna finish school. And I thank you for paying for my school and keeping me fly—I know you don't have to. I just wish you wouldn't let Dollar play you for a fool, that's all."

"He ain't playing me for no fool," I said. "He loves me and gives me the world. These bitches out here just dying to be me and live the glamorous life like I do. You just don't understand, cuz this shit ain't for you. You ain't gangster enough."

Sissy was just a good girl that wouldn't survive chasing money. That was why I made sure I kept her laced, so she wouldn't need to try to be like me.

"Well, I guess not, cuz I call what you're doing is being dumb!" she retorted.

"You know what, Sissy? This conversation is done. Don't worry about my business."

"Well, don't worry about mine either," she replied.

"I'ma worry about it as long as I'm taking care of you," I said.

"You ain't taking care of me. Dollar is. You ain't got shit but what he give you."

Sissy turned the radio back up, blasting Lil' Kim in my ear. I was pissed and ready to go back to my car before I beat the shit out of Sissy. She was lucky I loved her, or I would've been on Sissy's ass like white on rice. *I don't let these hoes get away with flip-*

ping off at the mouth at me. I know Sissy loves me and don't want to see me hurt, so I'ma let her pass, but if she keep on —

"Well, since I ain't got shit but what Dollar gives me, and he taking care of you, I ain't buying your ass shit out the mall," I told her.

"What?" Sissy exclaimed.

"Yeah, that'll teach you to keep your fucking mouth shut."

"Emerald, quit playing with me! I want a new Gucci bag!"

"That's what I thought," I said.

I loved Sissy to death and I'd beat a bitch down for touching her. She just didn't understand me, and she was right; I'd get her that bag, cuz I didn't want her out in the streets trying to get it. There was no need; I had money and she was my sister. *I'm all she got*, I thought. *It's my responsibility to make sure she straight, and she'll never have to want for nothing.*

Chapter 11
LEARNING THE BUSINESS

Money was pouring in for me like rain; my shit was flying off the shelves. As soon as I stocked it, it was sold. I knew I needed to do the right thing with my money, and I also knew that I wasn't sharing my shit with Dollar. I loved him to death, but shit, I feel like what's yours is mine and what mine is mine.

I opened me an account with Fifth National Bank. When I got my account, I met this cute Italian guy named John. He was tall and built. His deep brown eyes sparkled like my diamond Jacob, and when he smiled he had the deepest dimples you could find on a man. He was serious.

John came from a family that owned damn near everything, from pizza shops to car lots; even that bank he worked in. He was a businessman and he knew the ins and outs of retail. I was clueless on a lot of things, but he took me under his wing and showed me the ropes to running my business successfully. I knew he had a crush on me; he didn't have to spend as much time as he did showing me what I needed to do to get my business off the ground.

John knew that I hadn't finished high school, so he signed me up for a business class that I took every Wednesday and also a retail management class. John stressed the importance of my getting my GED, cuz I told him in the door that I wasn't going back to high school. I told him I'd think about it, but the way I saw it, I was doing fine without it. After four months of hanging with John, I learned so much about my business and making investments.

John was the same age as Dollar — twenty-five. I knew he liked me and wanted to get up with me. I liked him too; he was fine as hell and he always smelled so damn good.

John had all the right connections to get me to where I was trying to go. I talked to him about my plans and how I wanted my line to be as big as Baby Phat. He said he could help me with that and broker me some deals.

One day, I went to the bank to make a deposit; I had made ten grand in the last two days from my stores. John had also told me he wanted to meet with me about some business plans. I walked into his office and took a seat and waited for him.

When John walked in, the smell of his Issey Miyake cologne filled the room. "Emerald!" he said as he reached in and gave me a kiss.

"Hey, John." I blushed like a little schoolgirl.

"So, I wanted to meet with you to go over the plans for investing your money," he said.

I stared at John. He was looking so fine today. He always wore a three-piece suit. I'd never seen Dollar in a suit before — it just wasn't his style. John's Italian accent came across so smooth: when he spoke, you listened. He also talked proper. He was the total opposite of Dollar. I'd thought about getting up with him a few times. I'd always wondered what it was like to have sex with a white boy.

"Emerald?" he asked, breaking my concentration.

"Yeah?" I said, snapping out of my daze.

"Are you listening to me?"

"Yes. You said something about franchising."

"I did. My brother can help you. I told him about your returns — you've done very well in a short period of time."

John was right. I was clocking in mad paper, and I needed more space. "So, can we talk over dinner?" I asked.

"Sure. Your place or mine?"

"Yours," I quickly replied. Shit, there was no way his ass was coming to my place. Dollar would kill us both. Besides, I didn't want him in my business like that.

"Well, I'll see you tonight." John got up and gave me another kiss on my cheek, and I got up and left.

●●●●

I made sure I was looking dangerous when I went over to John's house. He had a condo right off Michigan Avenue, and when he opened the door for me, the smell of pasta hit me.

"What are you cooking?" I asked as I walked in and took a seat. John's house was nice: not as fly as mine but he had fixed it up nice. He lived in a much better area, though.

"Lasagna, my mother's recipe."

"So you cook? Where's your girl?"

"I'm single." John looked up at me with his dimples.

Right, I thought. John handed me a glass of champagne and motioned for me to follow him to the table. He pulled out my chair for me; I was shocked. Dollar never did no shit like that for me. I was skeptical about tasting the food at first, so I only got a little, but when I tried it, it was off the chain.

"Well, my brother sent over a business plan." John reached in his briefcase and handed me some papers to look at.

I flipped through them. His brother had spots for stores all over Illinois. The broker fee was small, and it seemed like a good deal. "How do I know you ain't trying to take advantage of poor little ole me?" I asked.

"Emerald, I wouldn't do that to you." John stared at me, deep into my eyes. I didn't know if it was me or the wine, but my pussy was flaming and calling his name.

I knew John had some great ideas for taking my business to the next level, so I was down for him helping me. "Well, John, the deal sounds great." I signed those papers knowing that this was my shit and Dollar didn't help me get nothing; I got it all on my own. It felt good to make such a good business decision without anyone's help. *People think I'm so stupid cuz I didn't finish high school, but I'll show them in the end*, I thought. *Once Icey blows up like Baby Phat, they gone be deep into my ass.*

When we finished eating and I was on my sixth glass of wine, Dollar was the farthest thing from my mind and I wanted to get a piece of John. I went over and sat on the couch next to him. I knew I was giving him some. *I'm horny, and Dollar's out of town anyway, and besides, he'll never know.* I leaned in and gave John a kiss on his soft lips.

He pulled away from me. "Emerald, I don't know if this will be a good idea."

"Why?" I asked.

"I don't want you feeling like you owe me something because I'm helping you."

"I don't," I assured him. "I want to do this." John didn't know shit about Dollar, and he didn't need to know my personal business.

I went back in and kissed him on his lips again. This time, he didn't pull away; he took his big hand

and rubbed it through my curly hair. I pulled off his shirt and threw it down to the floor. John's body was cut up hard like The Rock; he was solid. I got off the couch, removed my clothes, and pushed John down to the floor.

I licked him from his head down to his chiseled chest. He was moaning like crazy. I unbuckled his pants and his dick came flying out; it was much smaller than Dollar's. I looked up at him and smiled. *I hope he know how to use this little motherfucker*, I thought. I slid him deep into my throat. This was gonna be a piece of cake, getting him to be sprung out on my head; I could swallow his ass whole. I bobbed and weaved in a steady motion, making John scream uncontrollably. One I saw his toes curl up and his body tense, I knew he was coming. I pushed his dick so far down my throat, and his balls too. That was what you call super head. Ain't no bitch fucking with me; I'm the rawest.

"Emerald, my God!" John yelled out while his body was shaking.

Once I released him, John fell back, trying to catch his breath. I climbed up on the couch and put my pussy in his face; I wanted to see what his tongue game was like. He started to lick me softly on my bare pussy lips, and after five minutes, I got irritated. He didn't know what the hell he was doing. "John, put it in," I told him, cuz his tongue game was whack as hell.

After John banged me for twenty minutes, I climbed on top of him and made his toes lock. John's dick wasn't hitting on shit; he couldn't even compare to Dollar. This was gonna be the first and last time I'd let him get some.

John just stared at me. "You all right?" I asked him as I got up to put my clothes on.

"Yeah," he said. "Can you spend the night with me?"

"Naw, I ain't gone be able to do that. But I give you a call, though."

"All right, sweetie," John said as he planted a kiss on my forehead. I told John I'd holla at him later, and I meant that, all the way later; his dick was trash.

Chapter 12
HATERS

With the help of John and his brother I opened up two more stores in less than six months. I had mad dollars in the bank. I was known for more than being Dollar's girl: I was that bitch who owned them Icey stores. On the regular, it was always this young ho who came in popping her gums about how much she got from Dollar.

I wasn't in the mood for her shit, but I accepted everybody's money. I buzzed her and her tackhead friend into the store and they was popping their mouths soon as I let them in.

I looked at Ginger and she gave me a "let's fuck them up" look.

"Is there something I can help you with?" I asked.

"I'm just looking," she replied.

This young ho has been working my nerves, and whatever Dollar's giving her, she in my store giving it right back to me. Ain't that shit, gangster. "Well, the shoes in the corner are on sale, buy one get one half off," I told her.

She picked up a pair of my studded jeans and asked her friend, "You think Dollar would like my ass in these jeans?"

"Girl, you crazy," her friend replied.

"I think I'ma get these matching thongs for Dollar tonight."

I was over the edge. Motherfuckers was sleep on me, I'd slice a bitch about my dick. I saw her switching her stank ass through my store talking shit about my man. I grabbed a rhinestone thong and placed it to her face. "You know what? He likes these, so maybe you should try these with them red heels. He likes to see it like that."

She looked at me and frowned her nose up, surprised that I said anything to her. "I don't need your help." She smacked her lips.

"I think so. You riding a busted Cavalier, so I'm just trying to hook you to some game so you can least get a Honda Accord." Ginger laughed so loud that the young ho's face turned red. Her friend's expression changed to "let's get the hell outta here."

Dumb bitches that come in my store popping shit get treated. This young ho forgot that she needed to get buzzed in and out. "Yanna, I think we should go," her friend whispered to her, but it was too late. She was going to find out what I did to young hoes who can't keep their mouths closed.

"Ginger, should I show her how Dollar likes it?" I asked.

"Yeah, Emerald. Since she popping shit, I think you need to show her."

Her friend made a run for the door, but it was locked.

"Going somewhere? I'm bout to give you young hoes some lessons," I said.

"I don't have nothing to do with it," the friend said. I pulled out my .22 and pointed it at her head. "So, you bragging about fucking my man?"

"I ain't scared of you."

"Good." I pulled down my panties and sat back in my chair. "Since you want to pop shit outta your mouth, I'ma show you how to use it. Now you have two choices: one, I kill you and your friend, or two, you can eat my pussy. It's okay, you already tasted it many times before, since you fucking my man."

"Kill me then, bitch!" she yelled.

Ginger pulled the AK-47 from behind the counter and pointed it at her head. "Any final requests?"

Her friend was pacing the floor, crying yelling she didn't want to die.

"Yanna right, it's okay," I said. "It tastes really good. You have ten seconds to make your choice."

Ginger started counting down with that thang pressed against the ho's temple. By the time Ginger got to five, that bitch was down on her knees eating my pussy like her life depended on it. I let that bitch know that if she bit me she was gonna be dead. She was all right. She ate me until I came and than I made her eat Ginger's pussy too.

When she was finished, I played back a video-tape of her eating our pussies. I told her that if she showed her face again, everybody in the hood would know about her licking pussy.

I never heard or seen her since, and I never had another problem out of a hating bitch again.

Chapter 13
BROKEN PROMISE

"Wake up, Emerald!" Dollar yelled.

A quick glance at the clock told me it was only seven in the morning. "What's up, Dollar?"

"I need you to make a run for me."

"What?" I yelled as I tossed the blankets back off my naked body. "Another run?"

"Yeah. My little homey got locked up last night, and I need for you to make a run."

"Dollar, you promised me that you wouldn't make me do that again."

"I know. Shit happens."

"Well, I ain't doing it," I yelled as I pulled the covers back over my head.

"What you just say?"

"I said no! Ask S.L. to do it."

Before I could close my mouth all the way, Dollar had ripped the covers off my naked body and pulled me to the floor by my feet. I was scared. I'd never seen Dollar act this way towards me.

"Now, what you just say?" he asked with fire in his eyes. I was too scared to move or answer him. "I said, you gone drop this shit off and I ain't telling you again."

I sat on the floor looking up at Dollar, I didn't know this side of him and didn't want to know it either. He reached out to touch my face and I jumped back, scared of him.

"Emerald, baby, I'm sorry. I got a lot of stress, and I don't need you to turn your back on me now."

I just looked him in the eyes. I couldn't believe he'd just put his hands on me. He picked me up off the floor, got down on his knees, and licked me softly on my pussy. He was licking me and telling me how sorry he was for putting his hands on me. He'd never licked me like this before, I felt it in the way he touched me; he was sorry. "Emerald, I won't ever hit you again."

His tongue strokes went deeper into me; his lips felt so soft touching me. When he pushed his big dick into me, my body cringed. He felt bigger than normal. "Oh, Dollar," I moaned. He was working me right.

"You forgive me?" he asked as he kissed me softly on my lips.

"Yes," I moaned as a tear rolled down my cheek. I knew he was sorry and he was just stressed out. He was beating my shit up right, hitting all my weak spots. "Damn, Dollar!" I couldn't help screaming. He'd never hit it like this before.

After forty minutes of switching positions, we both fell to the bed to catch our breath. I just looked at Dollar. He was so fine and he was all mine; ain't no other bitch rolling like me. I got it made with my own money, a phat crib, and two fly whips.

I know the lifestyle Dollar lives. I know he has to make those drops in order to keep the money rolling in. I need to stop being a chicken and start being the gangster bitch he needs me to be. We in this together, Bonnie and Clyde. I'm about to be his ride-or-die chick.

Chapter 14
RIDE OR DIE

After the first five drops, it became a normal routine for me to drop the dope off. I wasn't scared no more. Dollar bought me a Cadillac truck with stash spots in it. The dope was well hidden, and even the few times I was stopped, I never got my car searched; just tickets from some assholes with nothing better to do. I felt unstoppable. After every drop, me and Dollar would make love on a bed full of money.

Money was everything, and I had the power! I was traveling Highway 90/94 with a quarter-million dollars twice a week. Dollar had a stash spot for that money, and he would only give me so much to clean up, which made sense. I still wasn't eighteen, and I already had four clothing stores, three apartment buildings, and a nightclub. Shit, life was good. It made Dollar love me even more to see me turn into his gangsta bitch. I was down for him. It didn't matter what he needed me to do; I was there.

Dollar taught me how to cook up the coke, and after a few tries I was a professional with it. I made local runs for Dollar when his street flunkies got locked up or put pussy over money. Dollar was the leader of the group. He already had two felony drug charges against him, so carrying the dope himself was not a option. I understood that and I didn't want my man to be locked up in a cage away from me. On the local drops, it was only dime bag shit, and I never worried about getting caught; Dollar's pockets was lined up with 20 percent of Chicago's finest. They knew I was his bitch, so nobody never messed with me.

●●●●

Sunday was the day of rest for me: I wasn't working or doing nothing for nobody. I was relaxing in the tub when I heard my cell phone blowing up. I paid it no never mind. I don't jump for no fucking body; they can wait until I called them back. Then the house phone rang, so that meant it was Dollar calling me on my off day. I got out of the tub, dried off, and answered the phone. "Hello."

"Bitch, why you not answering the fucking phone?"

"Who is this?" I asked. It sounded like Dollar, but somebody on the other end of the phone had lost their last mind.

"It's me. I called your cell phone ten times."

"I know. I was in the tub. You know, today is my off day."

"Get your ass down to the club now," he ordered.

"What's going on?"

"Them people here and they need to talk to you."

I knew exactly who they were. It was the police. "Shit, I ain't got time for this shit today."

I got dressed and made my way down to the club. When I got there, police cars were everywhere with that yellow tape they put down when somebody dies and a ambulance. "Emerald Jones?" a lady police officer asked me.

"Yes."

"I need for you to come with me."

I followed her inside the club, where I saw bloodstains on the wall and bullet holes. My heart fell. I didn't know what to think or what had happened.

"Ms. Jones, you are the owner of this club?" the officer asked.

"Yes," I replied. When we made it downstairs, I saw Dollar and S.L. sitting in the corner with handcuffs on. I ran to Dollar and gave him a hug. "Thank God you're okay!"

I turned to the policewoman. "Why are they handcuffed?" I asked her.

"Because I need to know what happened here."

I looked Dollar in the eye and he gave me that look that meant I should make up a lie. So I did.

"Some fool has been coming by here trying to break in. I filed a report with Officer Daily about this."

"When?"

"Last week and the week before that. It's been months, and you pigs don't move until somebody dies!"

"And the gun?" she asked.

"My gun is registered to me, and it was used to protect my business."

"You own a lot of things to be not eighteen."

"I do, I'm proud of that," I said. "Good credit can get you a lot. My mom passed when I was younger and left me a piece of change."

"Are you and Mr. Miller dating?"

"No. He works for my club, that's it." She eyed me and I knew she didn't believe me. But I didn't care; it wasn't nobody's business who I screwed.

"Well, when the gun checks out, they will be free to go, Ms. Jones."

"Thank you." I went to my office because all the blood was starting to make me sick to my stomach. Dollar had lost his last mind. I didn't know for sure what went down, but something had gone down.

Three hours passed and it was taking forever to get the gun information back. When I was walking out of my office, I saw them taking the cuffs off Dollar and S.L. I was glad this was over. I didn't know what else to expect.

"Don't leave town, Ms. Jones," the officer told me.

"Excuse me?"

"I mean, I might need to ask you more questions about tonight."

After she left, I looked at Dollar. I was pissed. I didn't have time for this shit. When we got into the car, I didn't want to look at him, I was so angry at him. I turned up my Beyonce CD, blasting "Me, Myself, and I," because the way I was feeling, that's all I have right now.

"Emerald, turn the radio down," Dollar said.

I did, even though I was pissed. I knew Dollar had another side to him that I didn't want to see. "Yes?"

"Look, I know you pissed, but you gotta believe me. I didn't know them niggas was gonna roll through there."

"I'm glad you okay, but now I got the police all on my back," I said.

"I know, and I'ma put in some calls soon as I get in to squash that shit. Don't even worry about it."

I knew Dollar was right. He had connections in the right places to make this problem go away. "Is there somebody trying to kill you or something?" I asked him.

"Baby, I'm number one in the streets," he said. "You gone always have somebody trying to take the top spot. But I ain't going out without a fight. Thanks for having my back, baby."

"Of course. Ride or die, right?"

"Right. Damn, I love my gangsta bitch."

Chapter 15
THREESOME

The police never came back to question me. Dollar handled that shit like he said he would. I went back to doing my normal runs and running my businesses. My eighteenth birthday was less than a month away, and I couldn't wait to turn eighteen; I would be officially grown.

I went over to see Ginger. It had been a month since I saw her, because they wanted us to lay low after the shooting. When I got there, her door was open, so I walked in and poured me a shot of Grey Goose. Then I went into her room and was surprised to see S.L. there. "Sorry, S.L.! I thought Ginger was here."

"She is," he said. "She in the bathroom."

I walked to the bathroom and found Ginger oiling up her long legs. "Why you ain't tell me S.L. was here?"

"Because he don't matter," Ginger said.

"Girl, he gone tell Dollar."

"No he ain't."

I gulped down my Grey Goose and walked out of the bathroom. "I'm out, Ginger."

I walked to the front room, and Ginger ran behind me. "Come on, Emerald, he just want to watch," she said.

This shit was getting too crazy for me. Ginger went to her bar, poured a drink of X-Rated, and brought it to me. "Drink this and relax."

I did. I washed down three glasses, and in a matter of minutes I was gone. Ginger came over, pulled down my dress, and began to suck on my breast. Ginger knew where all my weak spots were. Dollar was the last thing on my mind; I wanted Ginger to work that magic tongue she got.

When I looked down, all my clothes were off and S.L. was sitting on the edge of the couch rubbing on his dick. Ginger was naked and she had her face buried in my pussy. S.L. took off his shirt, and I'd never noticed that he had so many muscles. When he dropped his pants to the floor, I saw his huge dick. His dick was long and fat, bigger than Dollar's, and my eyes bucked wide open.

He pushed Ginger's ass in the air and hit her from the back while she continued to eat my pussy. She wasn't doing a very good job because S.L. was pounding her as hard as he could.

Then S.L. got up and put his dick in my face. At first I hesitated; then I thought about Dollar fucking my best friend and figured this would make us even.

I wrapped my mouth around S.L.'s huge dick and sucked the life outta him. Ginger began to eat my pussy at full speed. I made S.L. cum and he pushed Ginger to the side, stuck his dick in me, and started pounding me like no tomorrow was coming. For the next two hours we switched positions, partners, everything. It was one night to remember.

Chapter 16
DOLLAR

I laid low from Ginger and S.L.'s place. I felt like such a whore when I thought about what I'd done. My worst fear was that they would tell Dollar, even though they promised they wouldn't. I'd be lying if I said I didn't have fun that night, because I did. I had enjoyed the way S.L. fucked me. Besides, Dollar had that coming to him. I owed him one.

Now that I was eighteen, I could expand my business more. I wanted to open up three more stores; I wanted my clothing line to be as big as Baby Phat.

I had money stashed away that Dollar didn't know about. One thing Big Momma had taught me was to save and never let a man know how much money you have. I'd never forget that. Dollar didn't know about my bank account or how much money I was making. My statements went to a P.O. box; I didn't have to worry about nothing. All Dollar was worried about was running the streets and I was glad, he didn't notice that I had stores all over the place.

The store was slow today, shit I barely made one sale, so I closed up early. No sense in wasting money on lights and gas if ain't nobody coming in. When I was heading to my car, I heard somebody call my name. I turned around and bumped into the officer who had been at my club the night of the shooting.

"Ms. Jones, how are you?" she asked.

"Fine," I said, walking away from her. I don't like no pigs.

"Ms. Jones, I wanted to speak to you."

"Look, if you ain't charging me with nothing, then I ain't got shit to say to you!"

"Ms Jones, please, just a minute of your time," the officer said.

I stopped and turned toward her. "What?"

"I know you're dating Mr. Miller. You see, he preys on young girls like yourself."

"Excuse me. I'm eighteen, so it's nobody business who I give my pussy to."

"I know, Ms. Jones. It's just that Mr. Miller has a track record of dating young girls and setting them up to go to jail."

"Look, your minute is up." I jumped into my truck and took off. That lying pig had just worked my left nerve. If Dollar wanted me in jail, I would have been there. Police always try to use you and play mind tricks to get information. I might not have finished high school, but I ain't no dumb ho.

When I made it home, Dollar was there cooking in the kitchen. He had his shirt off and was looking extra-sexy. "Hey, baby, you cooking for me?" I asked.

"Yeah. I thought I'd fix you something today."

"Baby, you know you're too good to me." I didn't bother to tell Dollar what that pig had said, because I knew she was just lying.

"I ran you a bubble bath," Dollar said. "Tonight's all about you."

"That's what I'm talking about, baby." I went to the bathroom, got naked, and stepped into the tub full of bubbles and rose petals. Shit, my man be treating me right. The water felt so good on my skin.

Dollar undressed himself and got in with me. He massaged my feet, my legs, my back, every inch of me. Just looking at Dollar turned me on; he's a sexy piece of chocolate. A bitch will have to put me six feet deep to take him from me.

"Dollar, do you love me?" I asked him that from time to time to see what his answer would be.

"Yeah, I love you, Emerald."

"I just wonder sometimes, because of our age difference. Do I satisfy you?"

"Baby, age ain't nothing but a number. I'm happy."

"Well, I'm happy too," I told him as I moved to his end of the tub and kissed him. I slid down on his pole and started riding him. He felt so good to me.

Even though S.L.'s dick was bigger, Dollar knew all my spots, and he knew where to go to get my G-spot going.

"Baby, I want you to show me how much you love me," I said as I climbed up on the edge of the tub and threw my legs over his shoulders. "Show me how much you appreciate this pussy."

And he did. He buried his head into me and licked me so good until I couldn't take it anymore. After almost an hour of making love in the tub, we went to the bed and made love until we both couldn't take any more.

After eating the steak dinner Dollar had made for me, I fell asleep in his strong arms. I knew he wasn't playing me; I knew he really loved me.

Chapter 17
NO TIME TO WASTE

I didn't waste no time opening up my two other stores. Now I had a total of six stores all over Illinois, so I hired me an assistant because it was to much for me to handle. I knew damn well that I couldn't get along with no bitches, so I chose a gay guy instead. You know bitches can't be trusted! Ms. Peaches was a mess who kept me laughing. He was a nice-looking guy, too. It's to bad he got turned into a fun boy, he could'a been my dip.

"Hey Peaches" I said as I entered my store.

"What's up, bitch?" he asked me as he was popping his fingers to the stores loud radio.

"Nothing. Did the new shipment come in?"

"Yes, honey, and I couldn't wait for you to come in here."

"Why, something wrong?"

"Hell yeah! You ordered white jeans after Labor Day. What was you thinking?"

"Ms. Peaches, that's just a mind thing," I said.

"No it's not, and I hope you didn't order a lot, because it ain't gone sell," he said.

"Well, how come it was in my book to order?"

"For a sad soul like yourself to come along and get got."

"I think it's gone sell, Ms. Peaches."

"Honey, that's what I know is fashion. Maybe we can hold them until next spring, child."

"What about the other stuff?" I asked.

"Everything else was cool, especially the pocket logo jeans. My ass looks too good in them." He turned to let me see. "Catch the cookies, bitch."

"Ms. Peaches, you are crazy!" I laughed. "Did all the stores get their shipments?"

"Yeah, girl. And Dollar's fine ass stopped up here looking for you."

"What he say?"

"He said call him. Child, he fine. You think he'd let me hit that?"

"Ms. Peaches, hell no! And if he did there would be no us. He not gay anyway."

"Girl, it be them thug-out niggas that love to catch the cookies, honey. Don't be sleep."

"Well, throw your cookies somewhere else," I said. "Dollar's mine."

Ms. Peaches always keeps me laughing with his crazy ass. I called Dollar to see why he hadn't called my cell phone, but he didn't answer. His voice mail said his phone was broke, so I just left him a message. I guessed he was wondering about the drop for the next day, but I wasn't gon worry about it until I got home. I had to go over my books and make sure everything was everything.

After I made sure all my shipments were logged and tagged, I told Ms. Peaches I was leaving and to close up the store. Dollar hadn't returned my call, so I tried him back, but there was no answer again.

I thought I would stop by Big Momma's house to see what she'd cooked. I missed Big Momma's cooking.

When I pulled up to Big Momma's house, I saw Dollar's Yukon in her driveway. Then I saw Sissy jumping out of Dollar's truck. I pulled up behind Dollar so he wouldn't be able to pull out. Sissy was fucking Dollar! That's why she was always hating on him. Sissy was finna find out what I do to bitches that mess with my dick.

I jumped outta my car like Superwoman. "What the fuck is going on?"

Both Dollar and Sissy were surprised to see me. "Emerald!" Sissy said. "Girl, you scared me!"

"Bitch, I going to kick your ass if you don't tell me what the fuck is going on."

"Emerald, be easy. Dollar wanted me to go to the store to help pick you out something."

I shot my bloodshot eyes at Dollar. Who the fuck did they think they was playing? I'm hip to the game. "Bitch, I know that game very well," I said as I stepped into her face. "I know you fucking him!"

Dollar jumped outta the truck with a bag in his hand. He knew I will kick any bitch ass that came between me and my dick. I don't give a fuck about blood; that shit meant nothing to me.

"Emerald, here," he said as he handed me the bag.

I just looked at him and the bag. I knew in my heart he was fucking Sissy.

"Emerald, I was gonna ask you tonight," Dollar said as he got down on one knee. "Will you marry me!"

When I saw him open up a box with a ten-carat princess-cut diamond, my face fell to the floor. "Dollar, I'm sorry. I'm sorry, Sissy."

Sissy looked at me and rolled her eyes. "Everybody in this world don't want Dollar's stank ass!"

"I know. I was tripping. I'm sorry." I gave Sissy a hug and told Dollar that I would love to marry him.

I jumped into Dollar's arms. All my hard work had paid off: I was going to be Dollar's wife. Nothing could tear us apart. Whoever said dating a baller wouldn't be easy had lied; this was a piece of cake. In less than two years, I'd gone from being a Reebok vandal to rocking Chanel sandals. Every bitch in the hood was rocking my clothes and I had money in the bank. The life of a baller's wife would only get better. I mean, look at Ginger: she got it made. I was ready for Dollar to upgrade me to his wife and there was no time to waste. Dollar said his mother was coming for a weekend, and Ms. Price had always seemed nice over the phone, so I couldn't wait to meet her.

My blood, sweat, and spit had paid off. I was going to officially be Dollar's down-ass bitch.

Chapter 18
MS. PRICE

Dollar's mother, Ms. Price, stepped into our apartment dressed in a black Chanel pantsuit. My first impression of her was "money"; she represented Dollar well. She didn't look a day older than thirty-five. Her hair was a weave but well done, she was blacker than Crisco ass, and she had blue contacts in her eyes.

"Hi, Ms. Price," I said as I went to shake her hand.

"Baby, come and give me a hug," she told me.

I hugged her, and she smelled good, like White Diamonds.

"So, when the big day my son getting married finally?" she asked.

"Well, we haven't planned a day yet," I said.

"Well, if I was you, I'd go down to City Hall tomorrow and do it. You don't want to give a man time to change his mind."

I thought about what she said. She was right. I didn't want to give Dollar time to change his mind. "Maybe I will do that."

"You better."

Ms. Price proceeded to claim her territory. She put her things in the guest room, then went into the kitchen, pulled out my good pots and pans, and told Dollar she was cooking him a good meal. Like if he didn't eat good with me he ain't lost nobody's weight.

"Momma, you know I miss your cooking," Dollar gloated as he kissed his momma on her cheek. I just shot a dirty look at him. I can see now that Dollar was a mama's boy. I excused myself from the kitchen because I wasn't in the mood. I laid down on the couch and turned on BET to watch 106th and Park.

Then Ms. Price came and slapped my feet off the couch. "Girl, don't you have any home training? Didn't your momma teach you not to put your feet on someone else's furniture?"

I had to catch myself because I almost slapped that bitch. "Well, my mother passed when I was three and this is my home," I said.

"Honey, you're just a visitor until you get them papers on Vonzel. I'm sorry to hear about your mother. I understand why you would do such a thing."

I looked at Ms. Price I knew this was going to be a long visit. *Bitch, what you mean visitor? You a visitor, and if you don't watch out, your ass gone be on the outside looking in*, I thought. "I'm sorry Ms. Price. Me and Dollar been living together for two years and he never said anything to me."

Ms. Price just frowned up her face at me. That bitch don't know nothing about me. I'd slap the shit out of her and won't think twice about it.

"Dollar baby, Momma's been missing you," she said to Dollar. "You look like you lost some weight. This girl over here starving you?"

"She cook, Momma," he said.

"Um." She looked at me. "Well, Momma gone be here for two weeks, so Momma gone fatten you up."

I looked at Dollar. He'd told me she was gone be here only for the weekend. I don't know how much longer I can take her bullshit. "Well, Ms. Price, it was nice meeting you. I'm going to sleep." I got up, made my way to our bedroom, and closed the door.

I took a hot bath to relax me. I knew I had to get along with Ms. Price. Big Momma always told me that a man don't want a wife who don't get along with his momma.

Three hours later, Dollar came into our room and climbed into the bed. He rubbed his hand over my naked body, caressing all the right spots.

"Dollar, what about your mother?" I asked.

"So? How she gone know? This our house."

I proceeded to turn over and lick Dollar all over his muscles. His body always turned me on. I licked his thighs and put some hickeys on them. Dollar was moaning so loud; I kept telling him to be quiet, but he didn't care. I slid his dick into my mouth, deep down into my throat. I was reminding him about these young skills I had and the reason he wanted to marry me. I was talking shit to him, telling him to say my name. I was sucking him so good, and he was getting louder and louder. When he was about to come, he started pounding my face.

Before I could get him to quiet down, Ms. Price busted through the door and saw me on my knees with her son fucking the life outta my face. I tried to pull away from Dollar, but he was holding the back of my head too tight and I couldn't break loose until he was finished.

I slapped Dollar to get him outta his daze. His mother was just standing there giving us a nasty look, like she never sucked a dick before in her life.

"Would you two keep it down in here?" she said as she walked out with her hand on her hip.

I just looked at Dollar and laughed, then got up and locked the door. I slid down my man's dick, ain't nobody stopping my show.

●●●●

The next morning, when I was getting ready for work, Dollar was already up eating a breakfast his momma had cooked. I went over and took a bite of his sandwich, and his mother did not like it.

"Dollar, you shouldn't let people bite your food, especially when they do nasty things with their mouths."

"Well, make sure you don't eat behind Dollar or kiss him, if that's the case," I said as I shot her a smirk. I was glad to be getting outta that house. She was driving me nuts.

When I made it to the store, Ms. Peaches was already there; he was always on time.

"What's going on, Ms. Peaches?"

"Honey, you look terrible," he said.

"Thank you. Dollar's momma's here for two weeks, and she is working my nerves."

"Yeah, them bitches can be she-devils."

"Tell me about it. One minute we cool, the next minute she talking shit about me," I said.

"That's because you taking her baby away from her," said Ms. Peaches.

"Well, she better get used to me, cuz I ain't going nowhere."

"I hear you, honey." He held up a bank bag. "Where should I make this deposit for the store?"

"Ms. Peaches, can I trust you?" I asked.

"Yeah."

"Seriously, can I trust you?"

"Bitch, spill it!"

"Okay. I have a separate bank account set up for the clothing sales, and Dollar does not know about it."

"That's it?"

"Yeah."

"Bitch, I thought you was gonna tell me something good!" Ms. Peaches laughed.

"No, seriously, Peaches. Dollar can't find out about the money. I have it saved for just in case."

"What, just in case he catch these cookies? Cause I saw him eyeing me the other day, child."

"Ms. Peaches, stop playing with me." I was that bitch, young, black and hoodrich. I owned a chain of stores, and I was only eighteen. Dollar never questioned me about my sales; he didn't give a damn. As long as I exchanged his dirty money for clean money, he was all good. And I was glad it was that way; it was better for me to stack my paper.

Once we opened up, the store was packed because of our monster sales. I couldn't get a break. My feet was hurting something serious; this was the wrong day to rock my Manolo's. By closing time, I couldn't move a muscle. I just wanted to go home, get a foot massage, and lie down in bed.

I tried to rush home as fast as I could so I could relax and unwind. As soon as I hit the door, the smell of Pine-Sol hit me. Dollar's momma was tripping. That bitch had poured Pine-Sol all through my house, and her mouth was running a mile a minute.

"Dollar, I don't know how you could live up in this nasty house!" his mother was screaming. My nerves was bad and I'd just had a long day at work; I didn't have time for her shit. I gave Dollar that "you better get ya momma" look.

"Momma, you are a guest," he said. "Sit down and relax."

"Relax? How can somebody relax when this place is nasty?"

I walked straight into our room and slammed the door. Dollar came in behind me, trying to play things off. "My momma crazy, ain't she?"

"Crazy is a bit nice."

"She just wanna make sure you can take care of her boy."

"Well, I been taking care of you for the last two years, haven't I?" I asked.

"Emerald, just deal with her for a few more days and she will be gone."

I looked at him. "Um, so when we going to get married? Because I don't need a wedding. We can go to City Hall."

"We can go tomorrow when you come back from making the drop."

I was happy to hear that he was down for getting married so soon. Even though Ms. Price had worked my last nerve, she was right about waiting too long. I went to bed as Emerald Jones, but tomorrow when I lay my head down, I would be Emerald Miller.

Chapter 19
M.I.A.

Nothing could bring me down today, this was the happiest day of my life; I was going to be Dollar's wifey this evening. I slung that dope in my car so fast I could'a busted all the bags open. I wanted to get there and get back home as quick as I could. Wasn't nothing or nobody gonna stop me from becoming Mrs. Miller tonight. I listened to Beyonce's "I Rather Be With You" all the way there and back.

When I made it back, Ms. Price was sitting on the couch watching One Life to Live. I walked past her ass and didn't speak; she was on my bad side. I put the cash in Dollar's closet and went to the mall to buy something sexy for my wedding night. Tonight I was gonna make love to my husband for the first time.

●●●●

"Get your ass home right now!" Dollar yelled so loud through the phone that the whole store heard him.

"Baby, what's wrong?"

"I'm giving you ten minutes." Dollar slammed the phone down in my ear. I cut my shopping trip short because I needed to get back to Dollar to see what the deal was.

When I made it in the house, Dollar was pacing the floor. His eyes were bloodshot red. I knew he was pissed off about something. "What's the matter, baby?" I asked.

"Bitch, you stole my money!" he yelled.

"What?"

"I'm missing fifty grand, so where is it?"

"I don't know! I put the money in your closet like I always do."

Dollar turned and got into my face. I was scared outta my mind. "Didn't I give you everything, Emerald?"

"Baby, I swear on my life, I never stole nothing from you!" I cried as the tears started pouring.

"Then where's my money, Emerald?"

"I don't know! Maybe the guy didn't put it all in there."

"I thought you were supposed to count it before you left."

"I thought I did! What about your mom? Maybe she took it."

"You calling my momma a thief?"

"Dollar, I'm saying I'm not the person who took the money."

"My momma left this morning to go take care of my grandma," Dollar said.

This morning? I thought. *She was just watching* One Life to Live *a few hours ago!* I went to the guest room and opened the door. All Ms. Price's stuff was gone. I felt ill. That bitch had set me up! She took the money and ran off!

"What you looking up in here for?"

"Dollar, when I dropped the money off at two o'clock, your momma was still here," I said.

Dollar took his backhand and slapped me across the bed. "Bitch, you calling my momma a thief? She ain't got to steal from me."

"Dollar, please don't hit me!" I cried. "I swear I didn't steal it."

Dollar picked me up off the floor and punched me in the face repeatedly until blood gushed from my nose. I tried to get away from him, but there was nowhere to go. He choked me by my neck until I fainted.

I remember coming to with him pulling me off the floor, telling me I'd better get my ass out there and make his money back. "Dollar, what you want me to do?" I pleaded.

"Bitch, I don't give a fuck! Don't come back here without my money!" Dollar pushed me out the door and slammed it in my face.

I could barely see to get down the stairs because of my swollen eyes. When I climbed into my car, I thought about all the places I had to go. I couldn't show up at Big Momma's house. The only other place was Ms. Peaches' house, and I didn't know if he would have company or not.

When I rung Ms. Peaches' doorbell, I heard him yelling all ghetto. He peeped through and saw it was me, then opened the door right away. When he saw my fucked-up face, he knew that Dollar had kicked my ass good. "Girl, get your ass in here."

"Thank you, Ms. Peaches. I had nowhere else to go."

"Girl, what is Dollar's problem? You look like Martin on that episode he had that fight."

"Because he think I stole fifty thousand dollars from him," I said.

"What?"

"I know."

"Girl, did you tell that motherfucker that you got a half-million dollars in the bank?" Ms. Peaches exclaimed.

"No, I didn't. I'm just gonna take out the money and give it back to him."

"What happened to the money?" he asked.

"I think his momma stole it," I said.

"That bitch! You want to run down on her?"

"No. I need to find a way to give him the money back without him questioning me."

I laid awake that night from the pain of the bruises. My tears burned as they slid down my cheeks. Ms. Price played me. She stole the money and made it seem like it was me. Now I have to make it up to Dollar.

Chapter 20
PAYBACK

I laid awake all night thinking about how I could kill Ms. Price and make it look like a robbery. When I got up, Ms. Peaches was already up fixing breakfast.

"Girl, I fixed you some breakfast, honey. Your face looks a little better."

"It still hurts like hell."

He brought me a plate. "Girl, I'll run the store today. You just sit here and relax. Them bitches can't see your face like that, child."

"I know, but I have bigger problems."

"Girl, you need to call the police on his ass," said Ms. Peaches.

"I can't do that," I said.

"Why?"

"Because we live by the codes of the streets, and besides that, he got half the police in his pockets," I said.

"Whatever. What you gone do?"

"Take the money out the bank. My only problem is that if I give him all the money at once, he gone think I really did steal it."

"Girl, whatever you do, he gone think you stole it," said Ms. Peaches.

"I know," I said. "I could kill that bitch."

"Just tell him that you made this money from your stores and you had it invested to buy more. Make his ass feel real guilty."

Ms. Peaches had a point. I could get a check cut from my bank off my stock and give it to Dollar.

I wasted no time making my way to the bank. That was the good thing about having money. A lot of people think that just because you don't finish high school, you don't know how to make dollars and cents. Thanks to John my business had blossomed like a flower in the spring. With his help, I made all the right investments and my bank account was just as fat as my pussy.

I stepped into his office, took a seat, and waited for him to come in. I had packed my face with makeup and put on my big sunglasses to hide my swollen eyes.

"Emerald, how are you?" John asked as he took a seat at his desk.

"Fine, and yourself?"

"Great. I see the business is doing well; great returns on your money. What can I do for you today?"

"I need fifty thousand dollars withdrawn from my stock."

"Wow, that's a lot of cash," John said. "Is there something we can purchase for you? We can get it at a better rate."

"No, I need it as soon as possible," I said.

"Well fill out these forms." He handed them to me, and as I reached over the desk, he could tell from my motions that I was sore. My sleeve rode up and showed my recent bruises. "Emerald, are you in some kind of trouble?"

"No," I quickly replied. I didn't need him in my business.

"You know, I've been your banker for years now, but I thought we shared something close. If you need help, I can help you."

"Look, John, all we did was fuck, and that was long ago. I'm fine. I just need my check so I can go." I handed him back the signed forms.

He left his office and came back an hour later with a check. "Here, Emerald," he said, handing it to me. As I took it, he snatched my sunglasses off my face. "That's what you're hiding!"

I quickly grabbed my sunglasses and placed them back on my face. "Mind your business!" I screamed as I ran off.

●●●●

My feet were trembling as I walked up to Apartment 2C. I'd never had this feeling before. My hands were sweating and my mind was prepared for anything. I turned the key in the lock and opened it slowly. There was no sign of Dollar, so I opened the door wider and stepped inside.

There was a slight chill running through the place that made my nipples get hard. The same dishes were left in the sink and all the lights were out.

I walked into the bedroom and saw that the bed was messed up; that was typical Dollar. I needed to see Dollar. Even though he'd hurt me, I knew he'd only done it because he was mad. He had a lot of stress on him, and he depended on that money. Ms. Price was lucky she Dollar's momma, because she would've been rocked by now. She crossed me once. If she crossed me twice, I'll show her ass what I do to bitches that comes between me and my dick.

I didn't know if Dollar was still mad, so I called him private. "Who dis?" he said.

"It's Emerald."

"You got my money?"

"Yeah."

"I thought you said you didn't take it."

"I didn't!" I said. "I had some money from the stores invested and I took it out. Now I have nothing. This was all I had."

"Where you at?" he asked.

"At the house."

"I'll be home tomorrow." Dollar hung up.

I didn't bother to ask Dollar where he was at or who he was with. All I cared about was him coming back home and loving me again.

Chapter 21
THINGS AIN'T THE SAME

When I heard the door close, my heart started racing. I didn't know what Dollar was gonna do to me. He walked into the room and flashed on the lights. I had been sitting in the dark all night, so my eyes were blurry.

I quickly reached into the nightstand and handed Dollar the check. He took a look at it and smiled. "Emerald, you been holding out on me?"

"No, sweetie, that money is to keep the stock coming in. Now I don't have a dime to buy my spring collection."

"What I'm I supposed to do with a check?" he asked.

"Deposit it into your account." I was kind of happy that Dollar wasn't yelling and screaming at me.

He sat on the edge of the bed and looked at my face; because I'm light-skinned, you can see all of my bruises. "Emerald, this shit getting rough for me," Dollar said.

"Baby, I want you to know, from the day I met you until now, I never took your love for granted. I never stole a penny from you. Why would I steal? I've always asked you for everything I wanted and always got it."

"That's what I was thinking myself, but when my money comes up missing and it's only two people in the house—"

I wanted to tell him, "Three people, your stank-ass momma was here." Instead, I said, "Dollar, please take this money and love me like you used to. Like old times."

Dollar stared me up and down and stroked my bruised cheek. His touch felt good to me; I needed his touch. He leaned in and kissed me on the forehead. "Emerald, shit ain't working out."

"What you mean?"

"Me and you. We ain't working out."

My heart started racing. I saw Dollar's lips moving but no words was coming out. I went into a daze. I couldn't believe he was trying to break up with me. "Dollar, please, I'll do anything," I begged.

"Emerald, I can't trust you no more."

"Please!" I fell to my knees. "Don't leave me!"

"Emerald, just get your stuff and go," he said, pulling me off the floor.

My tears were falling a mile a minute. "Dollar!" I screamed as I reached for him. I fell to my knees again and started unbuckling Dollar's pants. I needed him to remember the reason why he loved me so much. I took Dollar in my mouth and started sucking him like never before. I needed him to change his mind. I needed him to stay with me.

I had him pinned to the bed so he couldn't move, and I was bobbing like no tomorrow was coming. His screams told me he liked it, but I needed him to love it. I needed him to scream it out loud to me and tell me he loved me and he was staying. I pushed his dick so far down my throat that I could have sworn he was in my ribcage. I worked all my throat muscles to make him feel good, good enough to want to stay with me.

"Shit, Emerald, I coming!" he cried out. I pushed him down my throat and stuck his balls in my mouth at the same time. I was sucking all of him, and he screamed so loud that I knew he loved it. When he busted in my mouth, I heard the magic words: I heard him say he loved me.

When I got up, I wrapped my arms around him and told him, "I can do you like that every day if you want me to."

Dollar pulled away from me and took two steps back. "So you really love a nigga?"

"Yes, baby, I love you. I'll do anything for you."

"A'ight," he said. "I need you to make a drop."

"Of course I will. I'll do whatever you want me to do."

"Cool. I need you to run to California, make a drop, and bring back the cash."

"No problem," I said. "What it gonna take, two days to drive there and back?"

"No. You catching a plane."

A plane? I thought. *What in the world type of shit is that, to get on a plane with some dope?* "Well, if you tell me what I need to do, I'll do it," I said.

"Cool," Dollar repeated. "You do that for me, and when you get back, we can talk about us."

I didn't question Dollar or pressure him into being with me. That night, I laid Dollar down and fucked the shit outta him. I fucked and sucked him until the early morning. I wanted him to know what I had to give him, and if making this drop was gonna pull us back together, I would do it.

Chapter 22
CALIFORNIA

I had some loose ends to tie up at the shop before I left. I told Ms. Peaches about the drop because
I knew I could trust him.

"Girl, I don't think you should go," he said.

"Ms. Peaches, would you stop already? I have
to go," I replied.

"What happens if you come back and he still
don't want to be with you?"

"He will."

"Girl, I know you been doing this for a while
now, but something don't seem right. I think he
setting you up."

"Ms. Peaches, just hold down the stores today. I
gotta go."

Ms. Peaches was always tripping about something. Dollar loved me; he was just pissed off about
his money. His momma was gone have hell to pay if
I came back and Dollar didn't want me. I had made
millions of drops before, so nothing was gonna
happen. I wasn't worried. Dollar had already told

me he put the dope inside the shaving gel cans, so I knew it wasn't gonna be a problem.

When I went through security, I put my carry-on bag on the table and walked through. I was finally able to exhale when I was cleared to get aboard the flight. I sat at the front of the plane by the door; I wanted to be the first person off.

The ride was smooth. It was my second time on an airplane, so I was a bit nervous. It was a six-hour trip, so I put on my headphones and closed my eyes.

When I heard the captain telling everybody to put on their seatbelts, I looked down and saw the Hollywood sign, and I knew I was in California. My plan was to drop the dope off, then go to Rodeo Drive and hit me some stores.

When I exited the plane, I did my power walk to the baggage claim to pick up my bags. I retrieved my belongings and made my way outside to catch a cab like Dollar had told me to.

When I got to the hotel, I went up to room 34A and tapped twice. A young Italian lady opened the door and asked my name.

"Emerald," I said.

When she let me in, I saw three guns on the table to the left of me and two to the right. I knew that this drop could go two ways: I'd get outta here dead or alive. I opened the suitcases and gave one of the shaving gel cans to the big gentleman in the corner. He popped the top and the foam busted out; so did the dope, wrapped up tight in a plastic bag. The smile that went across his face told me he was happy with the product.

The gentleman got up out of his seat and went to the back. He was gone for a while and I wondered what was taking so long. After ten minutes had passed, I looked at the Italian girl and told her I was leaving.

"He will be right back," she said. "He has to test the dope and see if it's good."

I just looked at her. Something in my gut was telling me to leave. I'd never had this feeling before, but I knew Dollar would be pissed if I didn't bring back the money. I had to stay because I needed Dollar to love me again and this was my only chance.

As soon as I sat down on the bed, the door busted open and the police swamped the place. My heart started racing and I blacked out. When I came to, I was in handcuffs getting pushed into the back of a police car.

My mind was all over the place. In all my drops, I'd never been caught, but now that I was carrying a half-million dollars' worth of coke, I'd gotten busted. I needed to call Dollar to come down here and bail me out.

When we got to the police station, I refused to talk until I got my one phone call. My first mind told me to call Sissy and ask her to do a three-way call to Dollar.

I was hoping Sissy would answer the phone, and she did. "Hello, Emerald? You in jail?"

"Listen, Sissy, I need for you to call Dollar on the other line and click us in right now." Sissy clicked over, called Dollar, and clicked me back in.

"What's up, sweetie?" Dollar said to Sissy.

"I got Emerald on the phone. She in jail."

"Dollar, I need for you to come and get me," I said.

"What happened?" he asked.

"I don't know. I think these guys were all police."

"What you tell them?"

"I ain't said nothing. I told them I needed to make a phone call, and I called you so you can come down here and get me," I said.

"Cool."

The line clicked off. I didn't know whether Dollar had hung up on me or my time had just run out.

When a lady detective came in to question me, I had nothing to say to her. I told them pigs I wasn't talking to them without a lawyer. She laughed her head off at me and I knew she was trying to get me. I was hip to the game: I watched Law & Order every week.

"Emerald, you know we can put you away for life," the detective said.

"That stuff wasn't mine." I knew they couldn't pin it on me because I had taken all my tags off the bags and I wore gloves the whole time.

"Why were you there?"

"Look, I'm not saying nothing until I get my lawyer."

"Do you think Mr. Miller will get you a lawyer?"

"I don't know what you're talking about," I said.

"Dollar," she said. "You see, Ms. Jones, we've been following you for a while now."

"Look," I shouted, "I ain't talking to you pigs until my lawyer gets here!"

"Fine," she said. "Book her."

The officer led me out, had them take my picture, and processed me in. When it was time for the strip search, I was unprepared for what was gonna happen. I got butt-naked and this old dyke bitch stuck her three fingers so far up my coochie I swore I was gonna start bleeding. They checked up in my ass-crack too. I felt violated.

When they pushed me into my cell and closed the gate, I felt ill. That night, I prayed to God for the first time. I needed a miracle. I couldn't spend my life up in here.

Chapter 23
WAITING FOR DOLLAR

I sat in my cell for three days, staring at the wall, waiting for Dollar to show up and bail me out. The police kept pressuring me to talk to them, but I didn't have nothing to say.

After a week, I started wondering if he would ever come to get me. When they told me I had a visitor, I jumped outta my bed in excitement.

I smiled and exhaled when I finally saw Dollar in the visitors' room, looking sexy as ever. "Dollar, what took you so long to get here?" I asked him.

"Man, I had to get some money together," he said.

"So what's the deal?"

"Well, I'ma get you a lawyer, but check this: they trying to pin this on me."

"So what you want me to do?" I asked.

"Look, I got two strikes. One more, I'ma go to jail for a very long time, Emerald."

"What does that mean?"

"Emerald," Dollar said softly as he rubbed the side of my face, "I love you. Do you love me still?"

"Of course I do, Dollar."

"My lawyer said that if you take the wrap, you'd only get one year in jail. I know that sounds like a long time, but you could get out in six months for good behavior. Then we can be together and get married and start a family and leave this life behind us. I love you, Emerald. Just think about me, you, and three kids and a dog."

I just looked at him. I couldn't believe my ears. He wanted me to take the stand and lie for him. Tears filled my eyes. I loved Dollar; I wanted to be his wife and have his babies. Six months wasn't that long to sacrifice to be with Dollar. I would'a stayed in here for two years, as long as he loved me and treated me like he used to. I knew that if I did this, I would win his love back and he would be able to trust me again. Our happy life would be back to normal, and I would be Mrs. Miller.

"I'll do it for you, Dollar," I said. "I'll do anything for you, Dollar."

Dollar reached over and gave me a hug and a kiss. I felt in the way he kissed me and held me close that he meant what he said. I knew Dollar had never stopped loving me.

"Fine," he said. "My lawyer going to meet you at the county when they transfer you back."

Dollar kissed me again, so passionately my panties got wet. Then he paid the guard two hundred dollars to watch the bathroom door while we went in to fuck. I dropped to my knees and showed Dollar how I'd missed my dick, and then he picked me up and fucked me like never before. I guessed he was giving it to me good because six months was a long time to go without having no dick.

When Dollar left, I wasn't sad. I went back to my cell knowing that six months later, I would be with my man again. I would be his wife: I'd be Mrs. Miller.

Chapter 24
THE COUNTY

My transfer back to the Cook County Jail was horrible. I was chained to the seat next to this big stanky-ass bitch. Her breath smelled like shit and she kept giving me the eye. Now, I know I get into bitches from time to time, but fuck, that ain't no bitch in here getting a lick of this shit.

I was looking forward to seeing Dollar in court. On the phone, his lawyer had told me he had everything under control. I felt comfortable with him; I knew I could trust Dollar's judgment.

When I met the lawyer, my first impression was that he had it all together. He called me into a room to go over the case with me before trial. He was a middle-aged white guy who spoke with a thick Greek accent.

"Emerald, I'm Attorney Davis," he said. "Take a seat."

"Where's Dollar?" I asked.

"It was best that Mr. Miller not show up today, because it would only hurt your case."

I was pissed. I'd been planning on seeing Dollar and now I was stuck without a kiss or nothing. "So what's gonna happen?"

"Well, you pled guilty to the charges for a deal from the state."

"What exactly are the charges?"

"No need to worry about that. I'll handle that end," he said.

"So, just say I'm guilty?"

"Yes," he said as he waved for the prison guard to come and escort me into court.

In the courtroom, I saw Big Momma, Sissy, and Ms. Peaches sitting in the audience. Sissy looked different to me: she had on a Gucci track suit, her hair was cut into layers, she had gotten blonde streaks, and she was iced out. I'd never seen Sissy dress that way before. Maybe I'd just been in here too long.

When they told me to stand up and asked me how I pled, I told them guilty. The judge asked me if I knew what I was pleading guilty to. I looked over at the lawyer to see what he wanted me to answer, and he nodded yes. I looked at the judge and a look of fear came over my face. The prosecutor told the judge to run down all the charges to me. It was a familiar voice, and when I looked over, I recognized the lady who had come to my shop questioning me about Dollar.

The judge looked at her and said, "Emerald Jones, you are being charged with fourteen counts of felony charges. Three counts are for illegal weapons possession, which holds a prison term of ten to twenty years. Eleven counts are for illegal drug possession with attempt to purchase and sell, which holds a minimum sentence of fifteen years. Do you understand these charges?"

My stomach went sour and I froze up and fainted. All I can remember is the prison guard yelling for help. My mind was wandering, but my body was frozen. Dollar had said six months, but that didn't sound like six months. Weapons? Where had weapons come from? I had to wake up, I had questions to ask Dollar.

When I woke up, I was handcuffed to the hospital bed. I looked around and my room was empty. I dosed back off to sleep until I heard somebody calling my name. When I opened my eyes, I saw the lady police officer standing in front of me.

"Are you okay, Ms. Jones?" she asked.

"I guess."

"Look, I'm not gonna bullshit you. We want Dollar. We all know that there's no way you could have done all that by yourself."

"Where's my lawyer?"

"If you're trying to protect Dollar, go ahead, but you'll end up like the other ones in the County who took up for him," she said.

I wasn't gonna snitch on my man. I didn't give a damn about what that pig was popping. "You don't know what you're talking about," I said.

"You know what kills me about Mr. Miller? He takes you young girls and screws your heads up. And you dumb hoes believe he loves you. He doesn't love you; he loves his money. While you're doing his time, he's gonna be on to the next one."

"That's not true!" I shouted.

"So you're willing to do ten years in jail for him?"

When she said ten years, things became very serious. In ten years, I'd be twenty-nine. I didn't want to spend all that time in jail and miss out on my life. "Well, I guess so, because y'all ain't catch me with no guns or all them counts of drugs," I said.

"No, we might not have caught you with it in your hand, but all those businesses you have in your name and those apartment buildings? You're the owner and you are responsible for what we find on your property."

I just looked at her because I knew she was right. Dollar sold drugs and guns outta all those places. "That don't got nothing to do with me," I said.

"Yes, it does. You see, the funny thing is that Mr. Miller pinned all of this on you. He said you were the queenpin in Chicago and the one who ran the whole operation."

One thing I knew for show was that these pigs be try'na lie all the damn time. They'll say anything to get some information up outta you, Dis bitch couldn't trick me. I knew Dollar would never say nothing like that. "I ain't got nothing to say to you without my lawyer," I told her.

"Fine, Ms. Jones. Maybe you should ask this girl named Angel on the inside about Dollar." She walked off and slammed the door.

I wasn't asking a bitch shit. Like she couldn't lie to get a lighter sentence. Dis bitch must'a thought I was a dummy with no sense. I don't believe nothing a bitch gotta say.

Chapter 25
WHAT'S REALLY GOING ON

When they released me from the jail's hospital, I was kind of glad to get unchained from the bed. My first stop was to see my lawyer; I needed some questions answered.

"Sit down, Emerald," he said.

"No, I'd rather stand. Now, please tell me, what's going on and why they charging me with gun charges?"

"I'm making a deal with the state to get those charges dropped."

"But why they pinning that on me?" I asked. "I didn't get caught with no guns."

"We all know that, but there were guns on your property. If nobody steps forward and claims them, they fall back on you," he said.

"Oh my God!" I screamed, going into a panic. "I need to speak with Dollar!"

"I don't think that's a good idea."

"Look, I don't give a damn! If Dollar don't bring his narrow ass down here today, he'll be going to jail right along with me!"

"I'll give him the message," the lawyer said. "See you in court tomorrow."

Mr. Davis got up and walked away. I went into my cell and waited for evening visitor calls.

●●●●

I paced back and forth in my cell. My name hadn't been called for a visitor. I was making myself even madder thinking about Dollar not coming to see me. Dis nigga done flip his wig. He trying to play me, I got that ass. I got so angry that I turned red and began to shake.

Twenty minutes before visiting hours were over, they called my name. I couldn't run down the hall fast enough. Dollar was sitting there G'd up and iced out while I was in that nasty-ass orange jump-suit.

"What took you so long?" I asked him.

"I got held up trying to get some money to put on your books. I still gotta pay your lawyer."

"Dollar, I don't think this gonna work out. They talking about guns and all these places I had in my name. The lady told me I'll be in jail for ten years."

"She just talking shit, baby," Dollar said as he moved closer to me. "They just trying to get you to tell on your man."

"Dollar, she told me there's other girls in jail that messed with you."

"That's a lie. Of course everybody knows who I am. Of course bitches got caught running that shit.

But you my wifey. I'm trying to get you up outta here."

"Dollar, I'm scared," I said.

"I know, Emerald. I got ya back. Even if it turns out bad, my lawyer can appeal it." Dollar hugged me so close to him that I heard his heart beat.

I loved Dollar's dirty drawers, I trusted him, I knew he had my back. He'd never done me wrong from the day I met him at sixteen. He kissed me softly on my lips and caressed my back in my favorite spot. "Don't turn your back on me now," he said.

I looked deep into his eyes. I wanted to see the love he had for me. "Don't hurt me, Dollar."

"I won't, baby. I'ma always be there for you. We forever right?"

"Right" I said. I got one final kiss from Dollar before he left, I missed him already, but dis is what this shit is all about. Ride-or-die I promised Dollar I was gonna hold him down. So I'ma hold him down. Six months is not that long I can do six months for my man; he'd sacrifice way more for me. I'm his Bonnie and I know my Clyde would'a done the same thing for me. I went to my cell and laid on my pillow, but I didn't go to sleep. I laid awake waiting for my judgment day.

Chapter 26
JUDGMENT DAY

I got called down for a visitor, and I thought maybe it was Dollar coming to wish me off. I was kind of happy that he'd come back to see me and let me know he loved me.

When I got there, it was Ms. Peaches, all dolled up. He came over and gave me a big hug.

"Hi, Ms. Peaches, how's the stores coming?"

"Girl, they running good," he said. "I got everything in order."

"Great."

"Emerald, you know I love you, and I tend to mind my own business, child. But you're in trouble, and since John had to straighten everything out with the stores, he said he got a lawyer that can get you off with no time."

"Ms. Peaches, I can't do that to Dollar."

Then Ms. Peaches looked at me like he never had before. He looked at me in the way a man would. "Emerald," he said in a deep voice, "this is Darrel talking to you as a man, so listen. Dollar is playing you! He used you and now he's manipulating you to get you to do his time in jail."

"Dollar wouldn't do that," I said.

"Girls like you come a dime a dozen to Dollar. You came from nothing and he gave you something. He wants you to feel like you owe him your life."

"I do!" I insisted.

"No you don't. He took your life and he's sticking you in here and then he'll be on to the next victim."

"I appreciate your concern, but Dollar's not playing me. We gonna get married when I get outta here. He promised me!"

"Bitches are so dumb sometimes, child," he said, flipping back to Ms. Peaches.

"Just promise me you'll watch the stores."

"I will, honey. God bless you, because you gonna be in here a while." Ms. Peaches walked outta the visitor's room and blew me a kiss goodbye.

When the guard brought me down to the courtroom, I was scared. I'd done a lot of shit in my life, and I'd never been scared, but right now I'm scared.

The judge's gavel banged twice to quiet the courtroom down. "Emerald Jones, please rise." I did, my knees were shaking. "I hereby sentence you to ten years in prison with a possibility of parole in six years."

After I heard "ten years," I passed out and fell to the floor. When I woke up, I was chained to the bed again and I started to hyperventilate. The nurse came in and told me to breathe into a bag. *What in the fuck did I just do?* I thought. *I'm in here for all my young years.*

I slept in my cell for weeks. I didn't go out once, not even when they tried to make me: I wouldn't leave. I didn't get a visit from Dollar and couldn't reach him by phone. I didn't know what was wrong. He had put five hundred on my books the last time he was there, but that was months ago. I was almost out of money. I'd been buying all kinds of magazines. I needed to try to keep my mind occupied because time is moving slow in here.

I wanted to speak to Dollar to see if he was working on a appeal for me so I could get out. Sissy hadn't come by to see me and the only things I got were weekly letters from Ms. Peaches and Big Momma. Sometimes I feel like committing suicide in here, but I ain't trying to go to hell. I needed to see what was going on with Dollar.

Chapter 27
NO CALL NO SHOW

It took forever for the morning to roll around. I wasn't staying in my cell today. I was going to make phone calls to try to get in touch with Dollar. As soon as the sun peeped through my window, I was ready for the morning calls.

"Everybody up and out!" the prison guard yelled.

I couldn't jump up fast enough. I ran down the hall because I needed to be the first person on the phone. Once I made it to the head of the line, I couldn't dial Sissy's number fast enough. I needed to see what the hell was going on.

Sissy answered right away. "Emerald, how you holding up?" Sissy asked.

"Bitch, how you think? I'm in fucking prison! Where the fuck is Dollar? How come he ain't put no money on my books or come and seen me?"

Sissy swallowed hard before she answered me. "I been trying to call him," she said in a low voice. "I don't know if he got lock up or not."

"Bitch, *what the fuck you mean you ain't heard from him?*" I screamed so loud my voice began to shake. "What about S.L.? You call him."

"Emerald, I done tried everybody," she cried.

"What?"

"I don't know what's going on."

"Call his momma right now!" I told her.

Sissy clicked over, called Dollar's momma on the three-way, and clicked me in.

"Hello, Sissy. Dollar ain't in," Dollar's momma said.

Sissy cut her off. "Ms. Price, I have Emerald on the line."

"What's going on, Ms. Price?" I asked. "I'm in here and I haven't heard or seen Dollar in three months now!"

"Baby, I ain't seen him either. I think he out of town. I'll tell him to come up there soon as he gets back."

"What am I supposed to do for money?"

"I got some," Sissy answered. "I'll put some on your books."

"Well, I need for you to come today," I said.

"All right. See you when I get there."

When I hung up on Sissy, I was pissed. Dollar's ass used me like Ms. Peaches told me. I went back to my cell and waited for visiting hours. It felt like days before Sissy made it to see me. They called me down twenty minutes before visiting hours were up.

When I entered the room, Sissy was standing there iced out. She had on the rawest BEBE outfit I'd ever seen. Sissy had never worn heels in her life, but now she was rocking six-inch Gucci stilettos. Her shy attitude had turned posse and cocky. She didn't have a hair outta place, her makeup was perfect, and she was rocking three-carat princess cut diamonds hanging from her ears. Her wrist was icey and she smelled great. Something was different about Sissy.

I went to give her a hug and she pulled away from me. "Emerald, please. I ain't trying to smell like prison."

It hurt me that she didn't want to hug me, but I understood. The smell in this place don't smell good. "So how much you put on my books?" I asked.

She looked at me and smacked her teeth. "Damn, bitch, hi to you too. I put four hundred dollars on your books."

"You look nice. What happened? You transformed from a old lady to jazzy."

"That's that hating shit you always been popping. I always been the shit."

Sissy's attitude had even changed. The way she spoke to me was to the left of our normal conversation.

"So you heard from Dollar?" I asked.

Sissy looked at me and frowned her face at me. "Look, Emerald, I'ma keep it real wit ya. Dollar ain't coming back."

"*What?*" I yelled so loud that the whole room turned around. My heart started racing.

"Emerald, don't act surprised. You know what you did."

"I don't know what you're talking about."

Sissy looked at me with disgust on her face. "You a tramp, bitch."

"What the fuck are you talking about, Sissy?"

"Dollar knows. As a matter of fact, he saw a tape of you fucking S.L. and Ginger. You dykin' now!"

My stomach went sour and I started shaking. Them bastards had taped that shit. "So what? He fucked my best friend," I said.

"And? You know that comes along with dating a baller. I told your dumb ass that before you moved in wit his ass."

"Sissy, what I'm gone do?"

"Shit, you gotta long time to think about it," she said as she busted out laughing.

I looked at Sissy. How could my own sister be so cruel? I saw her body motions; I peeped her steelo. She was fucking Dollar! "I'm glad that's funny to you," I said angrily. "Now I see, you fucking Dollar too!"

Sissy ran her hand through her freshly blowdried hair. "I ain't got to answer to you. But if you must know, I been fucking him."

I grabbed Sissy by the arm as tight as I could. I would've broken it, too, if the guards hadn't pulled me off her.

"Bitch, I ain't never coming back up here and putting shit on your books!" she yelled.

"He using you, Sissy," I said.

"Bitch, please! I ain't no dumb ho like you. I finished high school and I'm in college. He ain't using me: I'm using him."

"You knew he was setting me up!"

"Yeah, and you would have too if you took the time to finish high school," she said.

I was ready to snap Sissy's neck but the guard was holding me back.

"I hope that four hundred dollars gone last you ten years," she continued, "because you ain't got nobody now."

"Sissy, I'm the one who paid for you to go to school!"

"Thank you for that. Since I came down here and put some money on your books, I guess we even now." Sissy laughed at me like no tomorrow was coming. She turned her back on me and walked away.

"Sissy!" I yelled. "You can laugh now, but you'll pay later!"

"Bitch, please. By the time you get outta here, I'll be living in a Third World country. You don't have no money, so enjoy your time."

I just looked at her and smiled. *That's what she thinks. That's what they all think.*

Sissy switched her big ass outta the door, then turned around and screamed my name. "Emerald! I guess Dollar did want me after all!"

The guard took me away and put me back in my cell. I laid in my bed. My body was motionless. I had been played by Ginger, Dollar, and Ms. Price, but Sissy hurt most of all. She was supposed to be my blood. *They think they got me in here for ten years? I* thought. *Them bitches don't know I got a bankroll. My stores have been clocking in money; they ain't no nothing about me. Sissy think she smarter than me because I ain't finish high school? I might not have a degree, but I'm no dumb bitch.*

After I laid around for hours, my sadness turned into anger and rage. *That nigga done had me take the stand and lie for him? I'ma get that nigga back. I'ma get them all back!*

I called for the guard to come down and talk to me. Officer Linda was a dyke bitch who wanted to get a piece of my pussy, and today was her lucky day because I needed her help. I'm gonna bust outta this joint and get my revenge.

"Hey, what floor is this chick named Angel on?" I asked Officer Linda.

"She on block B. Why?"

"I need you to give her a message to meet me tonight in the laundry room."

"And how you gonna manage that?"

"You gone help me out," I said, giving her that "I'll let you fuck me" look.

"What you gone do for me?" she asked.

"Exactly what you been wanting."

Officer Linda licked her lips and smiled.

As long as her pussy ain't stanky, I'll break her ass off because I need her help. I'ma lick that bitch so good she gone fall in love wit me and do everything I say. She ain't my type of bitch, but beggars can't be choosy.

"Well, I'ma go tell her and I'm gone get you later," she said.

"Cool."

I laid back on my bed looking at the ceiling. First thing in the morning, I'ma call Ms. Peaches and tell him to call up the lawyer for the appeal. If I get this bitch Angel to trick with me, they should let us go. Or at least me. I don't give a fuck what they do wit her.

I let myself get screwed over, but never again, I told myself. Tonight I'm killing Emerald Jones and I'm becoming a new me. I'm becoming Shiesty. That's my new name, my new alter ego. Fuck being nice; fuck a nigga and a bitch. Shiesty ain't letting nobody run over her. I don't give a damn if you old, young, a baby. I don't give a fuck. You cross me, you gone get dealt with. Emerald died along with all that time she was dumb enough to take. Shiesty getting her ass outta here even if I got to dig a hole and get outta here. Motherfuckers about to respect my gangster, and if this bitch acting shitty, I'ma slap the fuck outta her.

Nichelle Walker

She got two options: you either rolling with me or you against me. But anybody rolling against Shiesty gone feel my wrath.

Chapter 28
ANGEL

I was depressed when I woke back up. The whole situation had become more real to me. Dollar had never intended to marry me; he knew exactly what he was doing. Now that I thought about it, I remembered that when Sissy called Dollar for me that day, he called her sweetie, and Ms. Price spoke to her like she knew her. It was all a setup. My own blood let a nigga come between us. They all sitting back drinking lemonade while I'm in here doing Dollar's time.

It's funny: I'd never thought I would end up in prison. Shit, I did floss like a boss bitch supposed to! And when I bust outta this joint, I'll be even colder.

"Emerald, you ready?" Officer Linda whispered to me, breaking my thought.

"Yeah, bitch, what took you so long?"

"I had to make sure the coast was clear," she said.

"Did you get her?"

"Yeah. She'll be down there in fifteen minutes."

Officer Linda escorted me back to the washroom that the guards used, locked the door, and pushed me against the wall. But I wasn't trying to let this bitch eat me; I just needed to use her ass real quick, so I pushed her off me and pushed her against the wall. "I hope your puss ain't stanky," I said.

"Hell naw." Officer Linda pulled down her pants, revealing her thong. There was no need to take it off. I pulled it to the side, dropped down to my knees, and began licking.

She was right: her pussy wasn't stanky, thank God. I knew I had to eat this pussy good like that bitch Ginger does me. I ain't worried; I'ma good fuck no matter if it's a bitch or a nigga. I licked, sucked, and played with her pussy for eight minutes before she busted. I knew I was good at what I do.

Linda tried to kiss me, but I had to let that bitch know to be easy. Ain't nobody trying to be in love with her ass.

Once she got dressed, she took me down to the laundry room to meet Angel. Angel was standing there with her back to the wall. She was a redbone with long Indian hair. She was very pretty—not as raw as me, but who is? She had a project tattoo of a dollar on her neck. Her body was fit, and she was a thick sister; I could tell she was mixed with something.

She stared me up and down, looking at me sideways. I could tell by her body motions that she was a hater. *Shit yeah, I look better than you. Don't blame me, blame your momma.* "So you used to fuck with Dollar?" I asked her.

"Yeah, before I got in here," Angel said.

"How long you been in here?"

"A year and a half."

"Shit, how much time you get?"

"Fifteen years."

"Look, I wouldn't mind staying here and shooting the shit wit ya, but I don't phony kick it," I said. "Dollar used me and locked me up in here, just like he used you. I got an appeal coming, and if you testify with me, they can let you outta here."

"I ain't got no money," she said.

"Don't worry about that. Is there anybody else in here because of him?"

"Yeah, his baby momma."

"Baby momma?" I knew she was flipping her wig. "He ain't got no kids!"

"Yes he do," Angel yelled as she rolled her eyes at me. I should've smacked the shit outta her ass for getting outta her body wit me. "He got a son, almost one, by this chick on cell block A. She got caught with some weed, so she ain't gonna be here long."

"Almost one? What's the bitch name?" cuz I couldn't believe it.

"Michelle. They call her Me Me. I only seen her once or twice when it's TV time."

My stomach cringed. That backstabbing bitch! So she still wanted to fuck with my dick after I kicked her ass, and on top of that he made me get an abortion and kill my baby because it was a girl. You know Emerald wouldn't even have cared about that, but Shiesty gone get that ass good.

"Look, Angel, me and you gone get outta here, but first I need you to get Michelle to come out for TV night next week. Don't mention my name, okay? I want to surprise her. She a old friend of mine."

Angel nodded. "Cool."

I was pissed, but the revenge was gonna be so sweet. "Look, I need to see the books and sign-in sheets right now," I said to Officer Linda.

Linda took me to the office and I went through the books. Dollar had just visited Me Me yesterday and put two hundred dollars on her books. The last day he'd came to see me; he saw her first; that's why I got called twenty minutes before closing. "Dirty bastard!" I said. "Linda, I need you to find out when this bitch getting out and I need a razor."

Linda didn't question me. She knew better. That bitch was finna pay the cost to be the boss. She was gone wish she never crossed me.

Chapter 29
NEW LAWYER

I called Ms. Peaches and it didn't take but a minute for him to call the lawyer for me. He was glad I wasn't being a silly bitch in love no more.

Mr. Meeks, the new lawyer, was a young sharp Italian guy. He told me my case was open and shut. I was too young to purchase all the property they were claiming was mine; by law, you have to be at least eighteen to establish any kind of credit.

Mr. Meeks advised the judge that I was scared of Dollar because he threatened to kill my family. He said I was only sixteen when Dollar manipulated me and he'd tricked me into confessing to things I wasn't aware of. When the judge asked him about the drop, Mr. Meeks said that the state had no evidence that I had brought the bags into the hotel room. He said I'd been there to purchase drugs because Dollar had me strung out, and I would be willing to attend rehab meetings to clear up my habit.

Mr. Meeks had all his ducks in a row. Angel's case was a little bit harder than mine because she was seventeen when she met Dollar, so she had to be accountable for all the things that were purchased after she turned eighteen. Mr. Meeks pled his case to the judge about Dollar using the both of us to do his time. He also had proof of three other women in prison in different states. He asked the judge to let Angel off with time served, since she had already done a year and a half.

I wasn't worried about the state's attorney fighting to keep me in jail. I cut a deal with them and told them about all Dollar's inside connections. I needed their asses up outta here so they wouldn't be reporting back to Dollar about me getting out. I didn't want nobody to know I was getting out.

When the judge told us to rise, my heart started pounding. This was it, either we stay or leave, but he continued our case until the next week. Mr. Meeks said that was a good sign and that the judge just needed to check into some things.

When I asked Mr. Meeks about payment, he said he owed John a favor, so I was taken care of. And that was cool with me. Shit, if he gets me outta here, I'll let him and John fuck me at the same time.

●●●●

When I got back to my cell, my bitch was waiting for me. She was starting to get on my nerves, falling in love and shit.

"How it go?" she asked.

"I don't know. I don't think it's looking good," I lied to her. I didn't need her nose up in my business trying to mess with my case so I could stay in here and lick her pussy.

"Well, I found out about Michelle," Linda said.

"Well, bitch, spill it."

"She ain't in here for no drugs. She sliced up a girl face over Dollar."

"Did she really?" That bitch had the nerve to be slicing bitches over my dick.

"Yeah. The girl who pressed charges against her just dropped the charges."

"So what that mean?" I asked.

"She'll be getting out next week," Linda said.

"Well, you get me the razor?"

"Yeah," she said as she handed me the razor.

"Good. I'ma send that bitch home looking nice and pretty for Dollar."

Chapter 30
ROXY

I bumped into this hood bitch named Roxy on my work detail. She was a lady Vice Lord, I had never met a real gangbanging girl before. Roxy's tried to be tuff but she knew not to pull that shit with me! Vice Lord or not I'd still get with that ass, so she knew better than to try to pull my card. She was a dyke bitch at that, the man kind. She always licked her fat-ass tongue out at me, and I wouldn't have minded her whipping her tongue game on me. I heard she can eat a mean pussy, but she ran her mouth to fucking much. Roxy was pretty but she tried to look like a man to much for me; she had a low-cut fade and everything. She was from out south, but she had connections everywhere.

Roxy wanted to tongue a bitch down she tried every chance she got, and I would've let her lick my puss, but she ran her fucking mouth too much and Linda's sprung ass would 'a found out. I couldn't take any chances to fuck up my hustle. I had some more time to do and I needed to use Linda's ass until I got out.

I went to do my work detail in the kitchen one day; they had paired me and Roxy together.

"Hey, sexy," Roxy moaned as she licked her lips.

"What's up?" I didn't feel like doing shit, and I wasn't. Those bitches could starve for all I cared. I jumped on the table and told Roxy I wasn't doing shit.

"I got the scoop on Dollar, girl!" Roxy yelled.

"What?"

"Nah, I don't think I should tell you."

"Bitch, you better spill it!" I shouted.

"Well, word on the streets is that he just copped him a big crib out there in Olympia Fields."

"Who gives a fuck?" I said. Roxy watched me trying to act hard. She knew I cared. My first mind wanted to ask her if Sissy was moving in with him, but I didn't give a fuck. It was going down when I got outta there.

"Right, you know I got some people that can handle Sissy on the outside," said Roxy.

"I'ma handle her ass myself," I said. "I don't need your help."

"All right, boo," she said as she stroked my face.

"Would you stop?"

"Why don't you let me break you off?" Roxy stuck out her long-ass tongue, twirling it around.

"Cuz you run off at the fucking mouth too much," I said.

"I ain't gone say nothing."

"Please," I said, rolling my eyes. I knew she was gone run and tell if she got a lick of this good shit. Who wouldn't?

"You just scared of me," she said.

I know she had me fucked up and confused, shit I ain't never scared. If she knew how to stop flipping at the lips so much, I would've let her break me off. Shit, I was horny anyway.

"Don't worry about Dollar," Roxy said, breaking my thought.

"What?" I snapped.

"My nigga Slim finna take over all his spots."

"Who is that?"

"My man from out south. He putting in work out here and he got the south side on lock, now he's working his way over to Dollar's turf."

"Slim, huh?" I made a mental note to pay Slim a visit when I got out. "What he look like?"

"He all right. You know I ain't into no niggas."

"So, where can I find him?"

"He goes to Neal's Car Wash on 59th and Racine every Friday at one. That's the best place to catch him."

I'm definitely seeing that nigga when I get outta here, I told myself. *Shit, if he can help me, good; if not, fuck it. Dollar's going down, with him or without him. He's gonna feel my wrath.*

I went back to my cell. I wanted to go to bed early; I had to meet a old friend tomorrow and get reacquainted with her. Me Me had crossed the wrong bitch.

Chapter 31
ME ME

Angel got word back to me that Me Me had told her she wasn't coming out for TV night. I knew Dollar had told her ass I was in here and she was scared. If *ya scared, go to church,* I thought. *That bitch gotta pay. Backstabbing trick.* I don't give a fuck about Dollar's ass any more, but it's the principle of the matter. I can't let backstabbing bitches get away with crossing me. I teach dumb ho's lessons, and class is in session.

I told my bitch to go down there and make Me Me's ass come outta there. I knew getting Linda on my side was a good move. At seven, that bitch ass is grass!

When the big hand hit the seven, the room was filled with bitches. They had *Three Strikes* playing for movie night, and I peeped Me Me looking around for me. I put my razor in my mouth and made my way behind Me Me. "Me Me!" I said, faking surprise. "Girl, what's up? I didn't know you was in here."

She turned around and screamed, "Emerald!"

"Girl, what you doing in jail?" I asked.

"Selling some drugs for these niggas around the way and got caught."

"Yeah, me too. So what's good? It's been awhile."

"Nothing. The same-old same-old," she said.

"When you getting out?"

"Girl, who knows." She looked away.

That backstabbing bitch couldn't even look me in my face. Dirty bitch. "Really, it's been years. You got any kids?" I was giving the bitch the benefit of the doubt to come clean to me.

"Nope," she lied right to my face.

I turned and looked at Angel. Me Me's eyes got big when she saw Angel walk over my way.

"Angel, Me Me said she don't have no baby," I said.

"Yes, you do," Angel said to Me Me. "You showed me a picture with you, Dollar, and y'all son."

Me Me just looked at me. She knew her ass was grass. "Yeah, I do." I saw the fear on her face. She knew I was going to kick her ass.

I hated to phony kick it, so I'ma keep it real with the bitch. "Me Me, you know I thought I beat your ass good the first time you crossed me, but maybe I didn't. You went and had a baby by my dick. You know you backstabbed me."

"Please, Emerald, Dollar ain't your husband."

"That's cuz I dismissed his ass," I said. "You a jealous bitch. You always been jealous of me. You ain't gone never look as good as me or fuck Dollar like me, bitch."

"Fuck you, Emerald!" Me Me yelled. "Dollar always wanted me! That's why I'm getting out tomorrow and you gone be in here for ten years. So if you gonna hit me, then go ahead. I'll be free as a bird tomorrow, sucking on Dollar's big nine-inch dick."

Before I knew it, I'd sliced up Me Me's face and lips with my razor and she had blood gushing from everywhere. I made sure I got that bitch good. I wanted that ho to have at least a hundred stitches. "Now fix that, bitch!" I shouted. Then I whispered in her ear, "I guess you won't be sucking Dollar's big dick, tomorrow or for a while."

I ran off to my cell and flushed the razor down the toilet. I went to sleep like a baby I didn't think twice about that backstabbing bitch. Sweet revenge feels good!

Chapter 32
FINAL DETERMINATION

When I woke up this morning, I wasn't even scared; I was happy. I had fucked that bitch's face up real good. Roxy said she looked like Chucky when she left. I wished I could'a seen the look on Dollar's face when he seen his trick-ass baby momma. I bet he leave her ass alone quicker than he came and got her.

The closer I got to the courtroom, the more my stomach began to turn. I was scared now. What if he say we had to stay up in here? When I walked in, Ms. Peaches was sitting in the front row, which made me feel much better. I prayed to God and asked him to let me up outta here.

When the judge entered the courtroom, things became more serious. I knew this was it. The judge asked me and Angel to stand. "Emerald Jones, what can you tell me that you learned from this experience?" he asked.

I looked at my lawyer. We hadn't rehearsed any thing to say. I wanted to say that the only thing I'd learned was to always put money over niggas, but instead I answered, "I learned not to trust people. I learned that a good education will take you anywhere you want to go. And I also learned to depend on myself and to take responsibility for my actions."

"Good, Ms. Jones. What about you, Ms. Davis?"

"I learned the same things too," Angel said. "And during my time in here, I completed my GED. If you release me, I going to school to be a chef."

"Ladies, I took into account all the evidence that was submitted to me. And in my reviewing, I do find that certain acts that you were convicted of were beyond your control. Since the state's attorney agreed to the appeal terms, my ruling today will overturn your sentences. Both of you will have time served thirty days from today. Thank you."

I didn't understand what he meant by time served or thirty days. I turned to my lawyer, who had a big smile on his face. "What does he mean?"

"He means that in thirty days you two will be free to go."

I looked at Angel and gave her a big hug. I'll be a free woman in thirty days! I looked at Ms. Peaches and smiled. "You gone be out there waiting?"

"Of course, bitch!" Ms. Peaches said.

When we went back to my cell, Angel didn't look as happy as me. "What's your problem?" I asked her.

"I don't have nowhere to go."

"You mean when you get out?"

"Yeah," she said. "I left my family for Dollar."

"Well, you can come stay with me," I told her.

"Can I?"

"Yeah, but before you make your choice, you see what I do to ho's who cross me."

"How did we fall for Dollar so hard?" Angel asked.

"Good dick, money, clothes, cars, trips...I could go on."

"Yeah, that nigga got good game. I feel sorry for the next dumb bitch he get with."

"Don't be," I said. "I'ma fix his ass. He'll pay."

Angel just laughed and went back to her cell.

I don't mind having Angel with me; she's a hot bitch. And when I step outta here, the new me steps in. I need a hot bitch on my team because I'm getting money when I get outta here. I'm getting revenge and money, and everything else can fall back. Shit, Emerald is dead and Shiesty is born. Emerald was a good bitch; Shiesty's going to be a paid whore.

I thought about all the money I made for Dollar and realized I was bringing him a half-million dollars every week. That was two million dollars a month and I didn't see one red cent of it. Never again. I ain't falling in love with a nigga next time around; I'm taking two to three dicks at a time. I'ma fuck who I want, how I want, and when I want. And dem niggas gotta pay me too. The last time I checked before I went to jail, Summer's Eve cost $3.49 a bottle, and I ain't douching my shit for the next nigga to bust a free nut.

Dollar ruined the good girl in me, and now I'm all about making a dollar. In one month, Shiesty is gone seek revenge on four ruthless motherfuckers: Sissy, Dollar, Ginger, and Ms. Price. They gone pay for what they did to me.

From all the bullshit I went through, I learned a few valuable lessons:

1. Never trust a nigga farther than you can throw him!

2. Sometimes blood ain't thicker than water. I came in this world by myself, and I'ma die by myself.

3. Payback's a bitch.

4. One rule every bitch in America should live by: always put **M**oney **O**ver **N**iggas!

Stay tuned, because in thirty days I'll be free and it's going to be the big payback. And I don't give a fuck about getting them back neither. They already know that when you live by the sword you die by the sword. Karma's a bitch: I learned that the hard way and so will they. When I step outta prison on August 01, 2007, I'ma have a new outlook on life. I'ma do whatever I want and live and die by my new rule in life: **Fuck niggas, get money!** I'll always and forever put *Money Over Niggas*.

Peace,
Emerald ;)

Stay tuned for the sequel

Excerpt From Upcoming Sequel

M.oney O.ver me.N
(When A Good Girl Turns Shiesty)

M.oney O.ver me.N
(When A Good Girl Turns Shiesty)

I had peeped Sissy's whole routine and she was biting my style hard. She was just a imitation of me; she was never gone be me even if she tried as hard as she wanted. That bitch would never be able to compare to me.

I'd been outta jail for a while now and it was time to put my plans in motion. Sissy and Dollar had a big house two doors down from R. Kelly. Wasn't that some shit? They got me in jail while they was out living like some ghetto superstars. I mean, they had a guard at the gate, acres of land, they was living big. *I should burn this motherfucker down,* I thought. *I'm the one who paid for this shit. I was the one running dope back and forward, and now the next bitch living good off my hard work.*

When I made my first appearance at Sissy's beautician, he couldn't tell us apart. I had another lady cut me some layers and streak my hair like Sissy's so that when I went to get my hair done by Sissy's beautician, he thought I was her. I was glad because that meant it was going to be easier for me to get her back. Everybody in there thought I was her; we do look just alike.

After the beautician, I made my way to their estate. I knew Sissy left for school at ten and she made it back home by one. That day, she had on a DKNY track suit and her hair was pulled back into a pony-tail.

I went and coped the same track suit from Macy's, took it to my hotel room, and changed. I pulled my hair into a ponytail Like Sissy's and put on my Gucci shades. She'd was carrying a Spy bag, which I already had.

I parked my car a block away and walked to the house. I was praying my plan would work, but I didn't know if I could fool the guards. When I walked to the gate, my stomach was turning.

"Ms. Miller, why are you walking?" the guard asked.

I looked at him. "Cause I wanted to mind ya business."

He opened the gate for me and I exhaled. I walked to the door and saw the gardener outside. "Senorita Miller, how are you today?" he asked.

I just looked at him because they all were pissing me off, calling her Ms. Miller. What, the bitch done married this nigga or something?

When I stepped into their crib, I was blown back. The house looked like paradise. It made his old apartment look like a project. There was a big-ass Tiffany chandelier hanging in the hallway and the spiral staircase leading upstairs was made of marble. I shot a look at the maid. "Senorita Miller, you're home early," she said to me.

Can you believe that? A maid. After I cooked every day of my life for that nigga, Sissy got a maid?

Upstairs there was a picture of Dollar, Sissy, and his bastard-ass son. The ten-carat princess-cut diamond on her ring finger confirmed that they were married. When I took a closer look, I realized it was the same ring Dollar had given me.

When I opened the French doors to the master bedroom, I saw more of the posh lifestyle they were living. I was there for a reason, and I was getting sick to my stomach, so I needed to leave. I reached into my purse and pulled out an 8x10 picture of me and Sissy at my birthday party. I searched through the dressers to find Sissy's and put the picture of us on her dresser. Then I heard footsteps coming, so I hid in the closet.

It was Sissy's closet and I was impressed: pretty nice. I peeped out and saw Dollar standing there with a towel wrapped around him. He was still built and looked sexy as hell. He looked over at my picture, took it off the dresser, and threw it in the garbage. Then he walked out of the room.

I ran out, took the picture out of the garbage, and put it back in the same place, then shot back into the closet and looked out. I didn't know he was gonna be there.

Even though I didn't want to feel this way about him, my pussy was wet just looking at him. I was having hot flashes thinking about how I used to put this pussy on him. I know Sissy ain't throwing her pussy like me. She was just a knockoff version of me and I knew Dollar missed this pussy. Shit, I had just fucked a nigga into love just yesterday.

Dollar went to Sissy's dresser, saw the picture was out of the trash, and looked around. "Sissy, are you home?" He touched my face in the picture, then dropped it back into the garbage. "Damn, Emerald, it seem like you here. Sissy, baby, you here?"

Dollar took his towel off and his dick was just hanging there, looking all tempting. I pulled out two scarves and Sissy's eye mask, then snuck out behind Dollar. I placed the eye mask over his eyes so he couldn't see me and pushed him down on the bed. I tied his arms over his head with the scarves, licked his chest, and sucked on his nipples.

"Damn, Sissy, you trying something new for ya man?" he asked.

I knew that bitch wasn't throwing her pussy like me. I licked him in all his favorite spots. "Shit, Sissy," he moaned. I was tired of him calling me Sissy, so I slapped the fuck outta him. *This ain't Sissy, nigga. I'ma show you who pussy this is in one minute.* My mind went to a place where I should beat his ass like ole girl did in *Diary of a Mad Black Woman*, but I decided not to. Dollar was going to get what was coming to him in due time.

I got undressed, took my panties off, and stuffed them into his mouth. I didn't want to hear him call me Sissy again. *Sissy ain't gone fuck you like this,* I thought. I sucked on Dollar's neck right behind his ear; that was his favorite spot. I licked every inch of him.

When it was time, when I knew I had him fee-nin for me to suck his dick, I shoved his dick down my throat to let him feel it for old times' sake. I sucked the life outta Dollar's dick, making sure I was getting him good. When it was time for him to bust, I slurped his balls into my mouth, flexed my throat muscle around him, and gave one powerful suck. The loud screams coming outta his mouth told me he was loving it. Shit, I knew he was; I am the baddest.

I climbed on top of Dollar and slid down on his dick. I rode him like a stallion. Shit, I'm a PDR, and for you slow bitches, that means professional dick rider. I bounced on top on him like no tomorrow. I was coming hard. I have to admit, Dollar's dick did feel good to me; I did miss it.

After I bust, I got off him with his dick still standing at attention. I whispered in his ear, "She ain't gone never be able to fuck you like me." I licked the side of his face and kissed him on the lips for the last time in my life.

I got dressed, took my picture back out the garbage, and put it on the dresser. I made my way outta his bedroom and told the maid that Dollar needed some help in his room. She rushed off to see what he wanted and I heard her scream, "Mr Miller, you're naked!" I laughed.

I saw Sissy coming up the stairs and she was right on time. I hid behind the column in the stairway. I heard her calling out to Dollar, but was she gonna be surprised when she got into her bedroom. Sissy busted into the room and all I heard was "bitch" this, "bitch" that as she yelled at Dollar for cheating with the maid.

My time was done here. There was so much yelling going on that the guards left their stations to see what was wrong. On my way out, I stopped at the security desk, pulled the tape out, and left unnoticed. I was happy with the outcome: I'd come to leave a picture and wound up getting a bonus. I got to bust a good nut; my day went well. I wasn't worried about Dollar thinking it was me. He got so many freaks he wouldn't know who it was.

The next time I come back, it's going to be hell to pay. Sissy was gone pay the piper soon.

Stay Tuned.
M.oney O.ver N.iggas
Coming Soon

Also Upcoming from NWHoodTales:

Excerpt From Upcoming Novel

Step Ya Head Game Up!

Step Ya Head Game Up.

Whoever said pussy is power ain't never lied. I found that out at the young age of eleven. I ran my finger across my clit slowly and got such a wonderful feeling. I did it again, but a little faster, and damn! A bitch was feeling like something was taking over my body. I didn't want that feeling to stop. I sped up a little faster and my legs began to shake. "Ohh," I moaned. Something was happening that I liked. Then a gush came out of me. I was too young then to know I made myself have an orgasm. I knew that if I could make myself feel good, I damn sure wouldn't have a problem making a man feel good.

Now I'm much older and I understand the meaning of "**Pussy Is Power.**" Men can't survive without it. Women definitely rule the world. I can fuck a man so good that he'd disown his mother, stop talking to his sister, and kill his brother if he thought he'd got a piece. Yup, pussy is power: you just gotta use it the right way. Giving boss head is a way to a man's heart, pockets, whatever. Head is the new pussy, so bringing your A game is a must every time. Boss head can turn the hardest thug soft in a matter of minutes.

Please believe me: if ya snooze ya lose. First impression means everything; ain't no room for half stepping. When you lay that nigga down for the first time, you better bring it. Let that nigga know you ain't the bitch from down the street or the ho from up the block. Show him you that bitch that's gone get him right; show him you dat boss *wifey*-type bitch! Let that nigga know ain't no need to keep searching, that you're definitely that girl he's been looking for!

It's just like a job interview. You say and do the right things to get the job. We have the power right in the palms of our hands, so don't be scared to use it. Use the powers that the good Lord blessed you with; don't run from it. Trust me, I know everybody ain't blessed by the good Lord to be a boss bitch, so if ya unsure or if ya brain game is lame, don't worry: there's always room to *Step Ya Head Game Up!*

Coming Soon to a Hood Near You.

Also Upcoming from NWHoodTales:

Excerpt From Upcoming Novel

Misery Luv's Company

Chapter 1
I GET IT FROM MY MOMMA

My momma was a fast ho. She started chasing money at thirteen. She met my daddy and let him run up in her pussy raw. I was born nine months later, but I was an only child, cuz my mother wasn't slaving for no kids. My daddy went in to do a bid, and my momma moved us from Kentucky to the ATL. When they sentenced my daddy to 25 years, she knew she wasn't waiting around for his ass. She moved us in with my great-grandma, cuz she was only fifteen and I was two. She still wanted to have fun and live her life. She was young, fly, and paper-chasing with the ATL niggas. She had all the hottest shit and she kept me fly. I always wanted to be pretty just like her.

I grew up so fast I never knew where the time went; I was seventeen in the blink of an eye. I called my momma by her first name, China. My momma and I were best friends; we wore the same clothes and looked like sisters. My hair flowed down my back and I had layers cut in it. My eyes were a misty green and slanted like my mom's, my skin was reddish toffee-brown like hers, and my body was vicious like hers. We had the same measurements — 36D-22-42, straight stallions, and stayed bossy. We was the baddest bitches in the ATL, hurting dem niggas' pockets hard.

It was my mother's thirtieth birthday, and she was having her party at Club 112. I was going to kick it with her. All I had to do was use her ID, cuz we looked like twins; they wouldn't know.

"Misery," my mom called to me.

"What, China?" I answered.

"What you wearing to my party tonight?"

"I don't know yet. Something hot, though," I said.

"You ain't found nothing?"

"No! I'm going out in a minute with Rell; I'ma pick up something then."

"Well, I hope your slow ass be ready on time, cuz I ain't gone be waiting for your ass today," she said. "Dis my day, not yours."

"Bitch, I'ma be on time."

"Good."

My momma could work my nerves sometimes. She never knew when to shut up and get in chill mode. All them niggas was coming out to see me, anyway. "China, I hope you ain't tell Rell about the party," I said.

She just looked at me and smiled. I knew her hating ass told them. She could be a cock-blocker sometimes. She knew Rell was gone be in my ass all night.

"I don't remember," she said.

"I just bet you don't. You hater."

"Hatin' on you? Please."

"Bitch, you is jealous of me," I said, and left. She'd pissed me off. Now I'd have that nigga in my ass all night long.

Stay Tuned.

Upcoming Titles
from NWHoodTales

- **M**.oney **O**.ver me.**N**!
- Lies and Secrets
- Misery Luv's Company!
- Step Ya Head Game Up!

About the Author

Author Nichelle Walker

Author Nichelle Walker hails from the fabulous city of Chicago. Nichelle found her love for writing early in life. During her high school years she penned several successful screenplays, short stories and her first novel. While matriculating through college to attain a degree in Accounting, Nichelle put her love for writing on the back burner only to find herself constantly wanting to write and tell her story. While on a three week break from school and unhappy with losing touch with her creative passion, she wrote her highly anticipated novella Doing His Time. Not wanting to wait on a publisher to decide her fate, Nichelle founded her own publishing company NWHoodTales Publishing. Nichelle Walker is excited to introduce her company and her novella to the world and show why her company's motto is "We Keep Them Pages Turning".

We Keep Them Pages Turning

Meet me at MySpace and let me know what ya think.
http://www.myspace.com/nichelle2007
Also hit me up at www.nwhoodtales.com

NWHoodTales

QTY	TITLE	PRICE
	Doing His Time $14.95/book	$
	Shipping & Handling $1.95/book	$
	***Discount if applicable	– $

Name: _____

Address: _____

City/State: _____

Zip: _____

TOTAL $_____

***NWHood Tales will give a 25% discount to all books shipped to a prison or county jail. Enter in appropriate line above.

Mail payment and form to:
P.O. Box 804782
Chicago, IL 60680